The Killer from Yuma

**Center Point
Large Print**

**This Large Print Book carries the
Seal of Approval of N.A.V.H.**

The Killer from Yuma

Lewis B. Patten

CENTER POINT PUBLISHING
THORNDIKE, MAINE

This Center Point Large Print edition
is published in the year 2008 by arrangement with
Golden West Literary Agency.

Copyright © 1964 by Lewis B. Patten.

The text of this Large Print edition is unabridged. In other
aspects, this book may vary from the original edition.
Printed in the United States of America.
Set in 16-point Times New Roman type.

ISBN: 978-1-60285-272-3

Library of Congress Cataloging-in-Publication Data

Patten, Lewis B.
    The killer from Yuma / Lewis B. Patten.--Center Point large print ed.
        p. cm.
    ISBN: 978-1-60285-272-3 (lib. bdg. : alk. paper)
        1. Large type books. I. Title.

PS3566.A79K43 2008
813'.54--dc22

2008016227

The Killer from Yuma

Chapter One

Traveling by night, she came across the baking desert out of the north, driving a dusty, creaking buggy and carrying a rifle across her knees. She could smell the river a long time before she reached it and could sometimes hear the baying of dogs, so faintly that the sound seemed born of imagination rather than reality.

Later, she came into Yuma, wearily glad to see the flickering lights in the windows of the squat, adobe buildings, glad to see other humans and to breathe the smells of habitation again, however unpleasant those smells might be.

The moon was up, and for several long moments she stared at the ugly, squared pile atop the bluff. This was the prison, Yuma Territorial Prison, and suddenly she was remembering all the things she had heard said of it. It was brutal and cruel and ugly, but it was not as much so as the renegades it housed. And it was feared—because too many of the men sentenced to it remained forever—in the graveyard beyond the prison walls that was almost as large as the prison itself.

She did not know how long this was going to take. A week, perhaps—or longer. The time did not worry her as much as the gnawing thought that she might not succeed at all.

And what she was planning might be terribly wrong. She shook her head impatiently and slapped her horse's back with the reins. Regrets and doubts must be left behind. She had chosen a course for herself and would now follow it to the end, whatever the consequences might be.

The horse plodded along the narrow, dusty street. She drew him to a halt before a low, adobe livery barn with an adobe-walled corral in the rear.

She spoke rapid Spanish to the Mexican youth who came out the door, then climbed stiffly down, holding the rifle in her hand. She took a small bag from the buggy and inquired briefly about a hotel. Then, following directions, she turned along the street toward it. The town was small and she reached the hotel in a few minutes and went inside.

Baked and burned and dusty, she stood motionless for a moment just inside the door. She was dressed in a soiled white shirtwaist and a dark-colored skirt of some heavy material. She wore scuffed, black, high-button shoes and a wide-brimmed man's hat, shapeless from many soakings, stained and streaked with desert dust and sweat.

Small, she was, but that was not the first impression she gave. Rather it was one of wiry and implacable strength. This impression was heightened by the intent and determined look in her eyes which were the color of the sky in the high country from which she had so recently come.

So dark had the sun burned her skin that her lips seemed almost colorless. Yet they were full and soft when not consciously compressed. A man might see beauty in this woman's face, but he would have to look beyond the marks that the desert and her present purpose had put upon it like a stain.

Again she spoke rapid Spanish to the middle-aged Mexican woman in charge of the hotel. She followed the woman up a narrow, dark stairway and into a tiny, oven-hot room at its head.

Patiently she listened to the woman's apology for the heat, to her promise of water and a tub with which to bathe. She watched the door close behind the woman, crossed to it and dropped the bar in place.

Only then did she relax. She leaned the rifle against the wall. The firmness went out of her mouth; the guarded, narrowed determination left her eyes. In this instant she was only a woman, alone in a harsh and savage place. She was a woman with an impossible task to perform who had no certainty that even its success would not be disastrous.

Cockroaches made a rattling, dry sound as they scurried across the floor. She did not lift her head or look at them. She crossed to the bed and sat down. She stayed there, unmoving, staring emptily before her until she heard a knock upon the door.

Her wariness returned instantly. She got up, crossed to the door and picked up her rifle again. She raised the bar and stepped quickly back, rifle at ready.

The door was shouldered open and the Mexican woman came in, awkwardly carrying an earthen jar of water. She went back outside and a moment later brought in a small wooden tub. She glanced at the rifle, then at the face of the woman holding it. She poured the water into the tub. Carrying the earthen jar, she went toward the door.

"Wait."

The Mexican woman turned her head.

"There is a man in Yuma that I must see. He is called Chavez."

"Many are called Chavez, senora."

"This one is called Pablo Chavez."

"Sí."

"You can get word to him?"

"Sí."

"I wish to see him tonight."

"Who wishes to see him, senora?"

"Tell him Donna Tate."

"Muy bien, senora." The woman went out, closing the door behind. Donna barred it, then began to strip the clothing from her body. Having done so, she stepped into the tiny tub, knelt awkwardly and began to wash.

Her youth was more apparent in her body than it was in her face and here no man would have had difficulty seeing beauty. Slender and strong, yet rounded as a woman's body should be, she was white and smooth from the sun-burned line of her throat to her slender ankles. Her breasts were high and full. Her waist was so slim that a man with large hands might easily have encircled it with the two of them.

She bathed quickly, apparently unaware of the discomfort of doing so in such a tiny tub. When she had finished, she dressed in the same clothing she had worn before, substituting only a clean shirtwaist which she took from her bag. Using a mirror also taken from the bag, she combed and put up her hair. Then she sat down to wait.

The lamp began to smoke but it was a time before she noticed it. When she did, she turned it down. Tension showed in the taut lines of her face, in her eyes, in her hands clasped so tightly in her lap.

Chavez would be her contact with the guard inside the prison who was known as "El Azote" or "The Whip." Inside her small bag, in addition to a few pieces of extra clothing and her toilet articles, was a thousand dollars in gold, which she hoped would be enough. It had to be enough, she thought with quiet desperation. It was all she had. In addition to bribing El Azote, it had to provide horses, and exchanges of horses along the way.

She waited tensely, and the hours slowly passed.

At first full dark, well before Donna Tate's arrival in Yuma, a guard came to the cell which Domingo Rodriquez shared with Owen Sands and with four others. His hoarse voice, recognizable as that of El Azote, came plainly through the double-barred doors. "Rodriguez. You are wanted for questioning."

Rodriguez shuffled obediently to the door. He heard the outer one swing open, heard the padlock on the inner door being removed. He stood quietly, waiting impassively.

The door creaked as it swung open enough to pass his body through. It clanged softly shut behind him and the padlock was replaced. He stepped out into the black corridor and waited until the guard had locked it as well.

He did not speak. Apparently his father's money had already spoken for him in the only language El Azote understood.

The keys jangled briefly and El Azote husked softly, "Come on."

He followed the guard along the corridor. Inside the insane cell he could hear the occupant whimpering softly to himself, like a dog in pain.

Next to it, the barred entrance to the room which held the dungeon was a blacker square in the blackness of the corridor. He would know what the inside of that awful pit was like, he thought, if he was caught tonight.

El Azote led him silently to the end of the corridor and right into the tubercular wing, thence outside into the exercise yard after first unlocking the barred door silently. He whispered hoarsely, "Go. There is a rope hanging from the wall. The moon will not rise for half an hour yet."

Rodriguez hesitated. Then he walked away, warily, across the exercise yard. He climbed the low wall and dropped to the ground on the other side. He could feel his heart beating wildly in his chest. Freedom lay on the other side of that high, thick, outside wall. In darkness he would be invisible to the guards in the towers. Once over, he could drop into the river and swim.

He glanced over his shoulder, half expecting some treachery from El Azote. But behind him all was still.

Warily he crossed to the wall. In the blackness, he walked softly along it, feeling its rough adobe surface for the rope El Azote had said would be hanging there.

He had gone two thirds its length and was beginning to wonder if this were not the way El Azote had betrayed him before he felt it in his hand.

He put his weight partially on it, making sure it was secured at the top. Having ascertained this, he kicked off his grass sandals and with his bare feet against the wall, began to climb.

Weakened by poor food, the blistering heat and the backbreaking toil inside the prison, he wondered if he would make it to the top. But the thought of freedom waiting on the other side gave him added strength. Panting noisily, he sprawled across the top, cutting himself on jagged glass and tangled wire but scarcely feeling the cuts.

When he had recovered from the climb, he pulled up the rope and dropped it on the other side. He glanced to right and left at the looming bulk of the towers, then slid down the rope to the steep, crumbling side of the bluff.

Making noise unavoidably now, he plunged down the side of the bluff toward the shine of the river beneath. When he reached the drop-off, he lunged out in a long, awkward dive.

His body made a thunderous splash as it struck the water. A rapid volley of shots racketed from above. He sank until he thought his lungs would burst, then came cautiously to the surface for breath and sank again. This time he swam strongly toward the center of the stream. When he came up a second time, he was a hundred yards away.

He could hear the shouts behind him on the prison wall and a chill of terror touched his heart. He swam until he thought exhaustion would take him and he would drown. But he reached the bank and crawled out on it. He lay panting there, waiting for his spent strength to return.

The night around him was still, yet it seemed to be filled with all manner of menacing sounds. If he could go a little farther . . . someone should be waiting for him with a horse.

Far behind him, he heard both the splash of oars, the creak of oarlocks, and the baying of dogs as they were given a scent of the sandals he had left inside the walls. Ice seemed to close around his heart. His breathing became shallow with fear and his lungs constricted with it. The Indians had those dogs. They would be coming soon in boats, with their uncanny endurance, their unbelievable skill. They would find his trail and follow it until they found him too.

He went back into the river and swam with the current, floating when his strength gave out, but he knew it would do no good. Unless he reached the place where his father's men were waiting for him with horses he was doomed. The Indians never took a prisoner back alive.

The moon came up, laying its cold shine upon the river and the land. Rodriguez came out at last, and lay spent on the muddy bank. The baying of the dogs came closer and closer still.

He got up and began to run again. He ran until he was exhausted, praying in desperation that he might see the figures of men and horses ahead. But he saw nothing. Nothing but emptiness and cold moonlight upon the expanse of sluggish river.

He could see neither dogs nor Indians yet, but they were very close. He stopped and stared ahead. He turned and stared behind. Then he looked at the river itself.

In this instant, he knew he had been betrayed and understood exactly why. No money had been paid by his father for his release, else his father's men would have been waiting for him with horses and food and water for the long trip south.

But the prison officials paid a bounty of $50 to the Indians for each escaped prisoner captured and returned. Or for each one killed.

Fifty dollars. Almost two months pay for a guard. El Azote must be working both sides of the street, letting prisoners escape, then sharing in the bounty paid the Indians for their return.

Rodriguez plunged toward the river, sick at the realization that he had fallen into their nasty trap. He knew now that he was going to die tonight. His life was worth exactly $25 to El Azote, the guard whose brutality had earned for him his name, "The Whip."

He heard underbrush crack as the dogs rushed toward him. He heard the sibilant swish of an arrow in flight and the sharp twang of a bow-string.

Something struck him in the back. Pain spread like fire in all directions from the spot. His head reeled and he plunged forward to land in the river shallows with a gigantic splash.

He was breathing water, and drowning, but his life was ebbing quickly too from the arrow wound in his back. His last choking breath was a curse for El Azote and a curse for himself as well because he had so foolishly fallen into El Azote's trap.

It was still midnight when the four Indians rode up to the main gate of the prison. One of them carried a grisly trophy in his hand. He dismounted and flung it on the ground before the gate. It was the severed lower leg of a man. Still in place around the ankle was the steel manacle with its ring into which a chain could be locked in place.

Lanterns and torches flicked weirdly. The guard on duty at the gate sent for the warden who came, accompanied by El Azote. There was no doubt as to the identification of Rodriguez's grisly remains. The shackle was evidence enough. And the leg was obviously very fresh.

The fifty dollars was paid and the leg removed for

burial tomorrow. The warden left and the guard on duty at the gate went back inside the small gate house. El Azote walked for a ways with the four Indians.

Money changed hands, clinking softly in the night. El Azote returned and re-entered the prison gate.

Donna Tate had heard the dogs and knew a prisoner had escaped. She did not know that he had been caught. Nor did she know what his price had been. If she had, she would have been more terrified than she already was.

Chapter Two

Donna stiffened as she heard steps on the stairs outside her door. She rose immediately, picked up the rifle and opened the door.

A man stood there, a wizened, dark-skinned man dressed in loose cotton trousers tied with a piece of rope, grass sandals and a soiled and well-worn shirt. He held a wide-brimmed sombrero in his hands. No weapon was visible.

"Senora Tate? I am Pablo Chavez."

"Come in." She stood aside and he entered almost timidly. She closed the door and stared closely at him for several moments, knowing she must trust him and trying to decide whether he would betray her trust or not. His trousers were a bit short and she could see the scars left on his ankle by a steel manacle. She asked, "You have been in the prison?"

"For two years, senora. I served my time and was released."

"I have been told that you know the guards inside. I have been told that if someone wishes to bribe them, you are the man to see."

"What do you want, senora?" There was sharpness now in his black eyes, and shrewdness too. He was obviously not as simple and ignorant as he appeared.

"I want a man. I want him to escape. I want to take him north with me."

"Your husband, senora?"

"That is not your concern. Tell me if you can get him out and how much it is going to cost."

"It can be arranged. For a thousand dollars it can be arranged."

Dismay touched Donna's thoughts. A thousand dollars was all she had. She shook her head and said firmly, "Two hundred. He is worth two hundred dollars to me and no more. If you cannot do it for that. . . ."

The man spread his hands eloquently. "It is dangerous, senora. More than one guard must be paid. I must have something for the risk I take. Perhaps for five hundred . . ."

"Three hundred and fifty."

"Por favor, senora . . . it is not enough. Perhaps for four hundred, though . . ." He waited expectantly.

Donna nodded agreement. Her chest felt tight and her throat was closed.

Chavez asked, "Who is the man?"

"Varra. Max Varra."

Chavez's eyes sharpened even as their lids pinched down. "That one?" He shook his head. 'I cannot get Varra for a penny less than five hundred dollars. You want the worst man in Yuma, senora. Why, I cannot understand. He will kill you before you have gone a mile with him. He would kill his own mother."

"I want him. I will pay the five hundred dollars, but no more. How long is it going to take?"

Chevez shrugged helplessly. "That I cannot say. He is in the dungeon, senora. He has been there for months. He killed one of his cellmates in an argument over a cigar."

Still holding his hat in his two hands, he said, "I will see. I will talk to . . . well, I will talk. I will let you know." He started for the door. Turning, he said, "I will need money now, senora."

"For talk?"

"Sí."

"How much money?"

"A hundred dollars, senora. It is the least. . . ."

"I will give you fifty. Wait outside and I will bring it to you."

He went out and drew the door closed behind him. Donna opened her bag. Reaching in, she opened the leather money bag inside and took out two twenty dollar gold pieces and a ten. She closed the money sack and then the bag. She took the money to the door, opened it and dropped the coins into Pablo Chavez's brown, thin hand. "When will I hear from you?"

"Tomorrow night, senora. I will come and report to you then."

Donna went into her room and closed the door. She stared around the tiny, oven-hot room in dismay. She must spend a week or more right here in this room, waiting, wondering, worrying. There would be no safety for her at any time. There would be less safety after Max Varra had made his escape and she had started north with him.

For an instant she thought of home, of the winy, cool, clear air, of the strong scent of pines in the breeze on a warm summer day. She thought of the green that covered the hills in early spring and of the blue and white of a tumbling mountain stream. She thought of the red shapes of cattle grazing, of a smooth and graceful deer spooking out of a thicket of brush ahead of her as she rode.

Suddenly, for the first time since her arrival, her eyes sparkled with hatred and her mouth tightened with anger. Max Varra was to be a tool of vengeance and retribution. He was the only tool capable of doing the job that must be done.

Do it he would, for his hatred was even greater than her own. But she knew one thing, and every time she thought of it, a cold ball of ice formed in her chest. He would do the job but he would probably destroy her too.

Right now she told herself she didn't care. As long as retribution was achieved.

• • •

El Azote came off duty at midnight. He came through the gate, a burly, hairy man whose head was bald and whose tiny eyes were close-set bits of ebony in a dark, unshaven face.

He paused as the gate clanged shut behind him, fished a cigar from his pocket and lighted it. He was thinking that Rodriguez's cellmates knew better than to tell the prison warden how Rodriquez had escaped. He was not called El Azote for nothing. Besides, they could not know that Rodriguez had been betrayed. They had no way of knowing that someone had not paid to have him allowed to escape.

He walked down the hill toward the town beneath. Gradually the stench peculiar to the prison faded from his nostrils, to be replaced by the stench peculiar to the town.

He turned in at the first cantina he reached, got a bottle at the bar and went to a corner table to drink. He sat down.

Pablo Chavez came in, shuffling and timid as was his way. He glanced at El Azote, then went to the bar, where he bought a drink of Tequila. Carrying it, he crossed to El Azote's table and sat down. He sipped his Tequila and said softly, "There is a gringo woman in town. She wants a certain prisoner to escape."

"How much will she pay?"

"Three hundred American dollars. It is much money for a prisoner, but this is no ordinary prisoner. It is Max Varra she wants."

El Azote scowled. "He's in the dungeon, for God's sake. How the hell can I get him out of there?"

"You will think of a way. It is better than the twenty-five you get from the Indians for. . . ."

"Shut up. How many times . . . ?"

"So." Chavez smiled mildly. He stared at El Azote, his face empty and bland. There were places on his back that still burned sometimes along the welts left by El Azote's whip.

The burly guard was a pig, a cruel, greedy pig who enjoyed the suffering he inflicted on the prisoners. Chavez hated him as he had hated nothing in his life before. There were times when he wanted to kill El Azote so much that he could scarcely restrain himself. Yet something always restrained him—the hatred itself, perhaps. He wanted more than El Azote's death. He wanted the guard confined to the prison as an inmate instead of as a guard. He wanted El Azote to know the misery and desperation that comes to a man when the heavy dungeon trapdoor clangs shut above his head. He wanted him to know the feel of the whip upon his back, as Chavez himself had known it. He wanted El Azote to faint from the heat in the burning sun of the workyard just inside the prison wall. He wanted him housed in one of the tiny cells with five others, each of whom had felt the bite of his murderous whip.

He stared at El Azote thoughtfully. Perhaps this particular escape could be so planned that El Azote would be caught and confined for his part in it. He asked softly, "How long is it going to take?"

"How the hell do I know? A couple of weeks, maybe."

"It must be sooner than that. No more than three days. The woman is nervous and afraid. She may leave without paying the money if it takes too long." Chavez was not afraid the woman would leave. He was thinking that a hurried escape could not be too well planned. If he rushed El Azote, there was a good chance he would be caught.

The guard shook his head, scowling. "It's too big a chance. They always tighten up for a week or so after a prisoner gets out. You should've let me know sooner. I could have kept Rodriguez until later."

"I did not know sooner. The woman only arrived tonight."

"Then let her wait."

"Perhaps her three hundred dollars will not wait."

El Azote's eyes turned sly. "For Varra I want two hundred and fifty of it."

"So. I will take fifty. But Varra is not to be caught by the Indians. He is to get away."

El Azote shrugged. "I can't help what the Indians do."

Chavez smiled. "But you can. Meet with them and pay them their twenty-five dollars in advance." He reached into his trousers and brought forth some gold coins. He laid a twenty and a five on the table. "For the Indians for not catching Varra."

El Azote took the coins, but he didn't speak. Chavez said softly, "Without me, my friend, you would have no gold put away against the time when you will no longer be a guard. This will be done my way or not at all. Do you understand?"

El Azote glowered at him. Chavez met his eyes steadily and it was El Azote who looked away. He grumbled unwillingly, "All right. All right!"

"Good. You will arrange it, then, for the night after tomorrow night. At twelve o'clock. That will give the woman time to procure horses and supplies. And it will give you time to see and pay off your Indians."

El Azote grumbled, but he agreed. Chavez finished his Tequila and rose. He walked to the door and into the night.

He knew he was playing a dangerous game that might easily land him back in the prison himself.

He also knew that this was the time. Varra was the most vicious of the vicious men confined up there. If Varra escaped, the man responsible for his escape would surely be sentenced to a term in Yuma himself. Chavez intended to see that the warden knew, in time to catch him at it if possible, who was helping Varra to escape.

Perhaps both Varra and El Azote would be killed. He didn't know. He could only hope that El Azote, at least, would live to learn the miserable difference between being a prisoner and a guard.

The grapevine at the prison was something no man understood. Perhaps men confined with nothing to do but think developed a sixth sense that makes the most of the small actions of guards and fellow prisoners. Whatever the grapevine was, it worked. By dusk of the following day, the word was being whispered around the prison that Varra was going out.

Owen Sands heard it as he was leaving the messhall, heading for the cellblock to be locked in for the night.

Whenever they left their cells, the prisoners were locked to a long length of chain, one behind the other and less than two feet apart. It was no different now. In step, as they were forced to walk because of the chain, they filed out of the messhall and along the corridor toward their cells. Faint gray light filtered in from the barred windows leading to the workyard. Farther along the corridor, torches in the hands of guards provided a yellow, flickering light.

Sands knew Varra was in the dungeon. He knew Varra was alone. If the grapevine was right and Varra was going out, then whoever was with him in the dungeon might also have a chance to get away.

There was not much time to decide—only the time it took to walk the dozen yards from the messhall door to his cell.

The line stopped as those leading it reached the cells where they belonged. One by one, they were released from the chain and allowed to enter their cells. When all six were in, the inner door and then the outer door clanged shut to be locked in turn.

Now only eight men were ahead of Sands. He felt his muscles tense. He knew he might be killed in the next few minutes but he discovered he didn't care. Not any more. Even death was preferable to three more years of this. Nor did he have any assurance that, sometime during those three long years, he wouldn't die anyway, of heat or disease as so many of the prisoners did.

El Azote held a torch in one hand, his whip in the other. Another guard was releasing the prisoners from the chain.

The line moved on, to the cell Sands occupied. Four men ahead of him now. One by one they went into the cell. And then, suddenly, Sands was free of the chain.

The guard who had released him started to rise and move back to the next in line. Owen brought his knee up and connected savagely with the guard's jaw.

The man was flung back against the door, which rattled with the impact. El Azote growled something indistinguishable and his whip lashed out.

Sands felt its brutal bite through his shirt, felt the shirt tear and the blood begin to flow. He lunged toward El Azote, to be met by a second vicious lash as El Azote backed away.

This one struck him full in the face, momentarily blinding him. He lunged on anyway.

From the chained convicts a low roar rose. From El Azote came a shout, angry yet alarmed as well. The whip lashed again, this time wrapping itself around Owen's throat. He clawed at it, even as it was yanked away.

His throat was on fire and he thought he was going

to choke. The door of the messhall slammed open and running feet approached along the low-ceilinged corridor. Swinging his head numbly, he saw more torches in the hands of the approaching guards.

He retreated toward the wall, to get it at his back. The whip, in the hands of El Azote, followed him, cutting, tearing, burning like an iron. He covered his face with his hands.

One of the other guards moved in, swinging a short length of chain. It collided with the side of Owen's head. He slumped and slid down the wall.

El Azote bawled, "Get away. Get away! I'll teach that son-of-a-bitch."

The others stepped back and El Azote stepped in. The whip rose and fell and rose and fell. The watching convicts winced each time it did. El Azote's eyes gleamed in the torches' light.

Consciousness slipped from Owen Sands. Yet in spite of the bleeding welts the whip had made, in spite of his other wounds, he knew that he had won. It was the dungeon for him. The dungeon was exactly what he had wanted and what he wanted now.

Chapter Three

Only half conscious, Sands felt himself being dragged along the corridor. He heard the outer door to the dungeon room being unlocked, and then the inner door. He was dragged into a room no larger than two of the cells placed together, in the center of which was a large trapdoor, re-inforced with strap iron exactly like that of which the cell doors were made. He was left for an instant, and three of the guards raised the door.

A stench floated up, of human excrement and sweat, a hot, fetid, gagging smell that made his stomach churn. One of them turned and kicked him in the ribs. "Get on down, you son-of-a-bitch!"

He crawled to the side and stared into the black pit. There was a ladder leaning against the wall. He eased himself over and began to climb down. The heavy trapdoor dropped into place, showering him with dust, plunging him into complete darkness.

He eased down, a careful step at a time. The hole was twelve feet deep and no larger than the trapdoor sealing it. He reached the bottom, feeling as though he couldn't breathe.

He heard the breathing of the other man, like that of an animal in its burrow. The floor was slimy and he almost fell. He moved across to one wall and put his back to it. He would probably have to fight Varra and he was in no shape to do it now.

He said softly, "Varra?"

"What?" The voice was hoarse, husky, as though it had not been used for months. Indeed it probably had not.

"The grapevine says you're going to be sprung."

The man crossed the hole like a tiger. Grappling, he seized Owen by the throat. Owen squirmed and fought, and because of the blood on his throat, suc-

28

ceeded in breaking free. He lunged across to the far wall and put his back to it. Varra spat, "Liar! You dirty son-of-a-bitch, I'll kill you if you're lyin' to me!"

"Maybe the grapevine's lying, but I'm not. Why do you think I'm here? I kicked up a fuss deliberately so they'd put me down here. I'm going out with you."

"Like hell you are!"

"Two men have a better chance than one. Rodriguez tried last night and he got caught. The Indians brought back his leg."

"Who would pay *me* out?"

"You know more about that than me. All I know is what the grapevine says."

For a long time he could hear Varra breathing hoarsely on the other side of the hole. He wondered if he could stand the stink down here until tomorrow night.

Other men, every one ever thrown in here, must have wondered that. He had seen men come out of this dungeon after being confined for months in it, their hair matted and caked with filth, their beards long and equally matted, their skins covered with running sores and scabs. He had seen them blink at the light and had seen the madness in their eyes.

He had also seen them lifted out, with ropes tied beneath their arms, and dragged into the corridor, dead. From disease or suffocation. From fighting like animals in this stinking hole.

Terror briefly touched his heart. What if the

grapevine had lied? What if something went wrong and the escape failed? There would be no retracting what he had done to get in here. He would stay until they decided to let him out.

Varra said something that Owen didn't hear. Varra shouted it a second time. "When? God damn you, when?"

"Tomorrow night." Owen's lungs were laboring. There wasn't enough air or else he was unconsciously breathing more shallowly because of the stench. What did it matter, when? Down here a man couldn't tell night from day. But he could number the days by the times he was fed. Twice every day a bucket was lowered on a rope, containing food and water.

He stood up as long as he could, not wanting to sit down. He heard Varra move, heard the rustling of straw. There must be beds of straw somewhere . . . .

He shuffled along the wall, kicking ahead of him with a foot. At last he encountered a pile of dirty straw. He sat down in it. He put his back against the earthen wall.

This part of the prison had not been built as the rest of it had, from adobe bricks and iron. This part had been excavated out of the bluff itself. The earth was an aggregate of rock and clay. A man might tunnel through it if he had anything with which to dig. But before he got out he would be caught because he would be unable to dispose of the earth. And he would stand in the sun at the post while El Azote laid on the whip. . . .

He closed his eyes. The bleeding welts burned like fire. His head ached terribly from the savage blows of the chain. When his eyes were closed he seemed to be floating, and turning, and sometimes falling too.

How little do men, free men breathing free, pure air, appreciate it, he thought. It is taken for granted because they have never known the horror of being without it. They curse the heat and the cold and the rain and wind. . . . He found himself remembering what it was like to ride a horse across the open plain with the warm spring rain beating down into his upturned face. He remembered the warmth of the sun upon his back afterward, and the pungent smell of dripping sage . . .

Varra began to snore. How, Owen wondered, could the man sleep, knowing escape might be near for him? He supposed the months in here were only made bearable by sleep. Varra had probably conditioned himself so that he could sleep whenever the darkness and the stench became too much to bear.

His own eyes remained closed, but he did not sleep. He thought of all the things a man had when he was free. Fresh air and cleanliness. The right to go where he pleased and do what he pleased. A drink when he wanted one. A woman. . . .

His heart thumped in his chest. How long since he had been with a woman? Oh God, if this was nothing but a hoax . . . If the grapevine had been wrong. . . .

The minutes dragged and the hours seemed like

years. But eventually the trapdoor above his head raised, admitting both light and a gust of air that by comparison seemed fresh and pure. A bucket came down on a rope and was seized instantly by Varra, who had sprung to his feet like an animal. Owen heard him gulping water from a can inside the bucket, then heard him greedily wolfing the food.

A second bucket came down. Owen drank the water, which was brackish and warm, and forced himself to eat the food. The trapdoor remained open while they were eating. Then the buckets were pulled up and it was closed, leaving them in darkness again.

The long wait continued, a wait that became more and more unbearable as the hours passed. Suppose nothing happened tonight? Would he be able to stand the disappointment, knowing he had gotten himself thrown in here deliberately?

He'd want to kill Varra, who sat hunched and silent and brooding on the other side of the pit. And perhaps he would. He didn't know.

Varra wasn't even human anymore, after months down here. He was a savage, who hated his fellow prisoners as much as he hated those outside the prison who had put him here. He lived for just one thing— the time he would get out, and go back, and kill everyone who had anything to do with his conviction.

For a time, Owen speculated on who it might be that was going to bribe Varra out of here. Some of his old friends, perhaps, men with whom he had associated. Perhaps Varra knew where loot from some hold-up was hidden and the knowledge was valuable enough to earn him help from outside the walls.

Supper time came and the door was opened again. Again the buckets were lowered in. Again the door was closed and they were left in darkness once more.

Owen prowled back and forth across the uneven floor of the pit. He counted the minutes and the hours away. When would it happen? Late, he supposed, after the prisoners were asleep.

Who would the guard be who came after them? El Azote, he supposed. The prison grapevine had it that El Azote was behind all prisoner escapes.

But there was one big question in Owen's mind that no amount of speculation could answer for him. How was he going to get out of here if neither Varra nor the guard wanted him to escape? There was but one ladder leading up and out of the pit. If Varra went out first, it would be simple enough for the guard to drop the door back down before Owen could crawl out on level ground.

He'd have to go out first, then, no matter what he had to do to make sure he did. If he went out first, the guard would have to wait and let Varra come up, for Varra was the one for whom the money had been paid.

Varra was growing restless now. He got up and prowled the pit. Owen put his back to the clay wall and waited silently. Varra would be up that ladder like a monkey the instant he heard the door. Unless Owen stopped him . . . Unless Owen stunned him long enough to get up the ladder first. . . .

He felt his way along the wall, halfway around the pit, until he felt the ladder beneath his hands. He stopped and waited, scarcely daring to breathe, hoping that Varra would not guess what his intentions were. He didn't want a fight to the death with Varra now. Not with freedom so very close.

He began to imagine what the fresh night air would be like in his choked nostrils, so fouled by the rotten air of the pit. He began to think what the sluggish, muddy water of the river would feel like against his skin, what a horse would feel like again between his knees.

He began to tremble violently. An intolerable tension came to him and grew until he thought he could not stand a minute more of waiting.

If they didn't come . . . he could feel unreasoning fury against Varra growing in his mind.

He heard a boot clang against the trapdoor immediately over his head. He heard something scrape—heard metal against metal as a crowbar was jammed beneath the door.

He should have thought of that. It took three men to raise the door. One would only be able to slide a bar in and raise it a few inches. It would be up to the prisoners to raise it enough more to squeeze on out.

He heard Varra coming and tensed himself. He wished desperately that he could see. But he could

34

hear, and he could smell. He could feel Varra move the ladder as he put his hands upon its rungs.

He lashed out with a clenched and bony fist. He knew it had missed Varra's jaw and cursed inwardly because it had. But Varra staggered back, choking and gagging, and Owen sprang up the ladder with desperate haste.

Reaching its top, he put his arms through. Using both arms and legs for leverage he forced the door upward enough to admit the upper half of his body.

He felt his ankles caught from below. He felt teeth bite savagely into his calf.

He grunted sharply with the pain and kicked. The hands fell away and he heard a thud from below.

He squeezed through and got unsteadily to his feet. He saw Varra's head and shoulders come through the opening. He seized the edge of the trapdoor and raised it enough to allow Varra to squeeze on through.

The trapdoor slammed as El Azote withdrew the bar. The man growled angrily, "Which of you is Varra? Damn it, I ain't going to take you both!"

Only a tiny amount of light filtered in through the double, barred doors, which were closed but not locked. Owen could see the dim shape of the guard. Varra snarled softly, "Shut up an' lay it out. Where are they going to be waiting with the horses? An' which way are we supposed to go out?"

"Through the consumptives' exercise yard. There'll be a rope hanging from the outside wall. Go into the river and swim downstream. They'll signal every five minutes with a lantern."

Varra said, "Who will?"

"I don't know. Now get going, will you?"

"In a minute, pig." Varra moved like a cat. There was a brief struggle, a sharp grunt of surprise from the guard, a sodden, dull sound of metal striking flesh. Then Varra had the bar and El Azote was on the floor. The bar raised and fell with savage regularity. . . .

Owen had been wondering how he was going to get up that rope before Varra did, and suddenly he knew. He opened the inner door and then the outer one as quietly as he could. He ran along the corridor in the direction of the consumptives' wing, hoping desperately that no outcry would be raised before he could get over the outside wall.

Chapter Four

The distance along the pitch-black corridor seemed to Owen like a hundred miles. He kept waiting for an outcry, for the thunder of shots. But no sound came.

He went out into the consumptives' exercise yard, opening the barred door with exaggerated care. Even so, the hinges squeaked. He crossed the yard at a crouching run and paused for an instant at the wall, staring toward the towers, one after another.

Hearing scuffing footsteps behind him, he vaulted over the wall. If he didn't reach the outside wall and find the rope before Varra did, he'd be left inside the wall, unable to escape, unable to go back. He'd either be killed or thrown in the dungeon again. . . .

His jaw hardened with determination. They'd have to kill him because he wasn't going back into that black, stinking pit.

He reached the outside wall. So dark was it that he slammed against it without seeing it at all. Desperately he moved along it, feeling for the rope. He hoped he had guessed right and that he was headed in the right direction. He hoped the rope was here and that this was not a cruel hoax perpetrated by El Azote . . .

He felt the rope, seized it and instantly began to climb. He heard Varra coming and felt the rope tighten as Varra seized it behind him and also began to climb.

It was hard to climb a tight rope, but desperation gave him the extra strength he needed for it. He reached the top of the wall and sprawled flat upon it. His breathing was hoarse and ragged.

Varra came over the edge and sprawled out similarly. Neither paid much attention to the glass and wire with which the top was strewn. Owen pulled up the rope and dropped it on the other side. It was anchored to a spike driven into the adobe wall. He tested the spike to make sure that it would hold. The climb had loosened it, but he had nothing with which to reset it and besides he knew he couldn't risk the noise.

He whispered, "Go ahead, Varra. Go ahead."

Varra eased himself over the wall and slid swiftly down the rope. Owen could hear Varra picking his way down the steep slope below the wall. He hoped the noise wouldn't be noticed, but he knew it had been when he heard a shout from one of the towers.

Owen let his body slide swiftly down the rope. He felt earth beneath his feet and plunged after Varra, guiding himself by the noise the other made. He heard a splash below and checked himself at the very edge of the bluff. Then he dived, forcing his body as far out into the river as he could.

Water closed over his head. It felt cold for an instant, but not for long. Holding his breath, Owen swam strongly underwater for as long as he could. He surfaced almost silently, took a breath and looked around.

There were torches on the wall and in the tower now. There was a rapid rattle of gunfire and the nasty splash of a bullet, not ten feet from his head. Farther out in the stream, Varra was swimming on the surface, noisily. Owen guessed they were shooting at the noise.

He submerged and again swam strongly until he was forced to come up for air. This time the torches were much farther away and the shooting had stopped.

But boats were putting out . . . he could hear the squeak of oarlocks and the slap of oars. He could hear shouting from the men manning them.

He swam on the surface now, following Varra who

was less than twenty feet ahead. Boats could go faster than a man could swim. It was going to be close. Everything depended on how far downstream they would have to go before they reached the place where horses were waiting for them. If it was very far, the boats would overtake them. But if it was close. . . .

He thought he saw a flicker of light on the far bank about a quarter-mile downstream. It was so quickly gone that he could not be sure, but he stroked almost frantically toward the spot. Apparently Varra had seen it too for his stroke picked up, becoming faster and even more frantic than before.

At least, Owen thought, if he died tonight he would die clean. He would die with the pure air of freedom in his lungs. He would die with the open sky above his head and clean, free earth beneath his feet.

He touched bottom with a hand, brought his feet under him and plunged through the river shallows toward the bank. A shot flared in mid-river from the boat. Another followed it.

The light again . . . a brief showing only and then it disappeared. Owen came out of the water and ran toward it.

Burrs and sticks and cactus penetrated his bare feet but he did not slow down. Varra ran immediately behind him, neither gaining nor losing ground.

Suddenly Owen heard sound ahead, the snap of a twig, the fidgeting of a horse, a soft wheeze. He slowed slightly and at a trot went the remaining distance.

There were three horses, two wearing saddles, the other a pack. Varra immediately seized one of the saddled horses and vaulted up. He thundered away.

A shadowy figure mounted the other horse. Owen vaulted up behind. The animal jumped and ran in the direction Varra had gone. The packhorse galloped along behind.

He could not believe it at first . . . this was not a man who had delivered them. It was a woman. Slight and small . . . his hand encountered a softly rounded breast and brought a gasp of protest from her lips . . .

The shouts diminished and died away. Varra slowed and Owen began to catch up. As he did, he whispered softly to the woman riding so close to him, "Don't say anything until daylight comes. If he doesn't know you're a woman . . ."

There was a fragrance to her, a clean, woman fragrance that stirred him tonight as nothing had ever stirred him before. He knew that if Varra realized she was a woman . . . He would stop. He would jeopardize the freedom of them all while he took her, with or without her consent.

Owen whispered, "Did you bring guns for us?"

"For him." Her voice was almost indistinguishable. "I didn't know there would be two."

"Give it to me."

She did not reply.

He said urgently, "Quickly! Now!"

He felt the cold grip of a revolver as she put it into his hand. Straightening, he slid it into his belt.

Varra pulled his running horse alongside. He yelled, "Got guns for us?"

"On the packhorse," Owen shouted. "Better make sure he doesn't fall behind."

Varra pulled away. He dropped a hundred yards behind and caught the packhorse. He stopped long enough to untie the lead rope from the pack, and then came on, towing the animal behind.

Owen slowed the horse he and the woman were riding. The animal was lathered and breathing hard.

Varra slowed his own horse as he came abreast. There was now no immediate danger of their being caught. Those who had pursued them in boats were afoot and constituted little threat. They would have to return to the prison across the river before a mounted party could set out. They might try trailing the fugitives in the dark, but it would be slow going. By dawn, the trio should have a lead of a dozen miles.

Cold terror had lived with Donna Tate for two days now. She had never really believed that Chavez could buy Varra out of the prison. She had expected to be betrayed, perhaps even caught and sentenced to the prison herself. She had heard that three women were confined there, and shuddered to think what they must be like.

Waiting in the darkness with the horses had been the worst yet—starting at each small noise, watching the gloomy pile across the river that was the Territorial Prison. Nor had she expected two men. And when the one behind her had put his hand upon her breast. . . .

Her heart thumped almost audibly in her chest. This aspect of the plan had not gone unnoticed in her thoughts. Men who have been confined for months and even years . . . became animals where women are concerned. Perhaps her worst hour was yet to come. But at least right now it was dark and they were riding hard and must continue to do so if they were to outdistance the pursuit.

Who was the man behind her, she wondered. He was big, and lean, and had the strength of . . . He understood Varra apparently. He had warned her not to let Varra know she was a woman yet.

Why? Out of concern for her? To keep her from being raped? She doubted that. There was no reason he should feel concern for her. He had never even seen her face.

His concern probably stemmed from the knowledge that they could not afford any loss of time, either for Varra to satisfy his appetite or for any other reason.

Maybe the man wanted her for himself . . . She shrank away from him suddenly, but she could not escape the hard, muscular pressure of his body from behind. His right arm was around her waist like a band of steel.

The terror she had felt before was mild compared to that she was feeling now. She felt as though she had loosed a tiger from its cage. Varra was probably the most vicious of all the criminals in Yuma and the other one might be almost as bad. There was a good possibility that when daylight came the two would take the horses and money and provisions and leave her naked and bleeding on the ground to die. She had no assurance that either man would feel enough gratitude to treat her decently or even let her live. The only thing that might make Varra do the thing for which she had obtained his release would be his own hatred and thirst for revenge.

She had been a fool. She knew it now. She had let hatred corrode her character until she was no better than the man she hated so desperately.

The horses were trotting steadily. The moon was up, and it laid a cold, weird light upon the desert and upon the tall saguaros with their ghostly, outstretched arms . . .

Desert animals scurried away from the horses' approach. An owl soared across the face of the moon. She was wet from contact with the soaking clothes of the man behind her and the night air of the desert made her shiver with a chill.

The man's arm tightened and he drew her closer against his chest. She felt as though she could scarcely breathe. When the sky grew light. . . . It would no longer be possible to conceal the fact that she was a woman from Varra any more.

She tried to remember what his face was like. She had been only fourteen when he had been convicted and sent to Yuma. That had been almost ten years before.

She couldn't remember him, but perhaps when she saw him in the light. . . .

A line of gray began to form on the horizon in the east. Her chest tightened and she could scarcely breathe. She closed her eyes and prayed silently, but she doubted if God would hear her prayers. Not after what she had done. She had loosed two killers, both of whom would kill and kill again before they were caught and put back where they belonged or hanged. There was a price on what she had done and when dawn came she would begin paying it. In pain and degradation. Perhaps even in death.

Gray spread slowly across the sky. She could feel Varra staring at her now but she didn't look at him. She began to tremble and however she tried, she couldn't stop. Her body felt like ice.

His eyes . . . they seemed to burn her where they touched. His voice was hoarse and ugly when it came. "Hey, by God! It's a woman! An' you been sittin' there pawin' her all night!"

The man behind her said, "It's a woman, but I haven't been pawing her."

Varra pulled his horse close. He reached out a hand and tried to slide it into the neckline of her blouse. The man behind her reined sharply away. Donna's trembling increased.

Varra's voice turned thick with anger. "You son-of-a-bitch; you wasn't supposed to get out with me at all. Now you're tryin' to hoard that woman like she belonged to you. Well she don't, understand? We're

44

goin' to stop right now because these horses need the rest. An' when we do . . . well I'm goin' to have somethin' I haven't had for damn near ten years." Varra talked as though he were short of breath. Donna glanced at him.

His eyes burned like coals. His mouth was tight with strain. His hand, holding the reins, was shaking violently.

She remembered him now, remembered that face, creased with lines of callousness and cruelty. It was bearded, and older, but if anything the man's character was written in it more plainly than it had been ten years before.

The horses continued to jog along. Donna's trembling continued. She closed her eyes again so that she would not see Varra's face but it was painted permanently on her mind and she could not shut it out.

Even if the man behind her felt disposed to defend her from Varra now, he couldn't go on doing it forever. He had to sleep sometime. When he did, Varra would kill him with as little feeling as he would experience stepping on a scorpion.

Varra's voice raised, and it came out almost like a scream. "Stop, you bastard! Stop that god-dam horse! I've waited long enough!"

Chapter Five

Donna felt the horse on which she was riding drawn to a halt. She opened her eyes. The man behind her dismounted, but he held onto the reins as he did. She looked at his face.

It was a lean, angular face belonging to a man in his early thirties, she guessed. His eyes were blue, a faded shade of blue, and were surrounded by a thousand tiny wrinkles formed, perhaps, from squinting against the unbelievable glare of the Arizona sun. He wore a prison uniform from which the three upper buttons were gone and she could see his chest, covered with fine yellow hair. His trousers were short enough for her to see the manacle and the scabbed sores it had made on his ankle.

She said desperately, "There are clothes on the pack-horse. And a hacksaw to cut your irons."

He nodded curtly, his eyes on Varra. He said, "Get the clothes and the saw. Let her alone."

"Like hell!" Varra rode close, licking his lips. Donna snatched for her rifle in the saddle boot and slid it out. It was wrenched from her hands by the man on the ground.

She was defenseless, then. He did not intend to defend her nor did he mean to let her defend herself. She stared down at him, her eyes suddenly brimming with tears. "Please. Please. . . ."

Varra dismounted. He released his horse and lunged

46

toward her. He seized her ankle and yanked her from the saddle. She fell on the hot sand and the fall temporarily knocked the breath from her.

He was on her like an animal. His hands ripped the shirtwaist from her with one yank. He seized the waistband of her skirt. . . .

She heard a sound immediately above her head and caught a glimpse of a man's bare foot. Varra rolled off. The other man's voice said harshly, "Damn you, I said let her alone!"

Donna crawled toward her torn blouse. She felt the eyes of both men on her. From a corner of her eye she saw Varra move, and cringed.

He was not moving toward her but toward the other man. He lunged upward, digging his bare feet into the hot sand. The other backed away, her rifle in his hand.

She reached the blouse, snatched it and put it on. Whatever happened, there was no hope for her now. It was only a matter of time until one or the other of them would get his hands on her. No one could help her out here, alone with this savage pair.

Varra growled between his teeth, "You son-of-a-bitch, I'm going to kill you, the way I ought to have killed you before you even got over the wall."

She watched dully. The first man was backing, the rifle held in front of him. Varra shuffled in pursuit. Obviously the first man didn't want to shoot and Varra knew he didn't.

They moved in a semi-circle for twenty feet. Suddenly Varra lunged. He reached the other man and

47

grappled for the rifle. It came around in a short arc, the barrel striking him on the side of the head.

Varra slumped, partly conscious, to the ground. The other man turned his back and walked toward the horse carrying the pack. He asked, "Where are the clothes you said you had?"

She got up unsteadily. "On this side. I'll. . . ."

She heard Varra coming. She caught his movement from the corner of one eye. Then she saw him, a rock fisted in his hand, lunging toward the man fumbling in the pack.

She screamed, "Look out!" and the man swung around. He was too late to completely avoid the blow, but he ducked enough so that it struck only a glancing blow. He slumped beneath the pack animal's hoofs and the horse danced nervously away.

Varra ignored the rifle and swung around, grinning in a strange and ugly way. He said, "Now. . . ."

Donna glanced at the man on the ground. He was still conscious, shaking his head as though trying to clear it. Blood ran from an abrasion on the side of his head.

Donna ducked behind the packhorse. She was smaller than Varra, and quicker on her feet. But she knew her breath, her strength would give out before his did.

If she could keep away until the other man regained his senses . . .

Varra began to curse, and each curse made her wince. He lumbered around the horse doggedly, sometimes stopping unexpectedly and reversing direction.

Donna felt sobs choking her. And then, suddenly, the other man was up and his voice was like a whip. "Varra!"

Varra stopped and Donna veered away from the packhorse and ran across the desert for a couple of hundred yards. She stopped and stared back at the pair.

They were talking but she could not understand their words. And then, suddenly, Varra lunged at the other man.

They stood facing each other, slugging it out ferociously, for what seemed an eternity. Even at this distance she could hear the meaty, solid sound as each blow struck. Sometimes one or the other would stagger away, but neither went down.

At last Varra turned and plunged away, toward the rifle on the ground.

She caught herself praying soundlessly—for the other man—until she realized what a blasphemy it was to pray for either of them.

While Varra was still a dozen feet from the rifle, the other man caught him and struck him a long-swinging blow that hit him on the side of the neck. Varra went to his knees.

The other man's knee came up. . . . Varra fell flat on his back and laid completely still.

Donna returned timidly. By the time she reached him, the man was sitting on the ground working at his manacle with a hacksaw. He glanced up at her, then back at his work. One of his eyes was turning black and his mouth was cut and bruised.

Donna went to the packhorse. Standing behind him, she changed her blouse. She returned. The man was pouring a canteen sparingly into Varra's upturned face.

The man opened his eyes and rolled, choking and cursing. The man corked the canteen and tossed the hacksaw down at him. "Here. Get busy."

Varra sat up, glanced at her and then at the other man. He said softly, "I'll kill you, Sands."

Sands didn't reply. He went behind the packhorse. Donna could hear the sounds he made as he shed his prison uniform and put on the clothes he found in the pack.

Varra glanced up from the manacle at her. His voice was hoarse and she couldn't tell what emotion, if any, it revealed. He said, "What's your name?"

"Donna Tate."

"Jake Tate's girl?"

"Yes."

"You was only. . . ."

"Fourteen. When they sent you to Yuma."

"Yeah." His voice seemed to be habitually harsh.

Her hands were clenched. She bit her lip until it bled. This was fantastic, incredible. A few moments before he had tried to rape her and now he was talking to her as though nothing had happened at all.

The rasp of the saw continued. Sands picked up Donna's rifle from the ground, then returned to the

50

packhorse and began going through the pack. He hefted the oak casks of water slung, one on each side, to make sure they were full. He refilled the canteen from one of them but he did not drink.

The sound of the saw stopped abruptly and Varra's manacle clanked as it dropped to the ground. Varra stood up, crossed to the packhorse and found clothing for himself. He stripped in front of her, watching her as he did, but she turned her face away. Sands said, "Let's get going. We've wasted enough time here."

He helped Donna mount, then swung up behind her. Varra mounted and led out, trailing the packhorse behind.

They rode in silence across the baking heat of the desert. Horses and men, and Donna too, sweated helplessly. Dust rose from the hoofs of the two horses ahead, settled on Donna and mixed with the sweat. It caked like a mask on her face.

Sands asked hoarsely, "Know this country at all?"

"I came this way."

"Any ranches where we can get fresh horses?"

"Yes. The first is about fifty miles from Yuma."

"Are we headed right?"

"Near enough. We go through that cut in the mountains up ahead."

Sands lapsed into silence. For a while they rode without talking. The sun beat down upon them mercilessly. Donna's mouth felt like cotton. Her lips cracked and began to bleed.

At last Sands asked, "Why did you get him out?"

She didn't answer immediately. She had been thinking about that. She had also been thinking of all that lay ahead of her. She could feel her composure slipping. Her knees began to tremble violently. She bit her lip fiercely and clenched her fists. Behind her Sands said in his deep and suddenly gentle voice, "Easy. Easy. I won't let him get his hands on you."

She asked bitterly, "Why? So you . . . ?"

He was briefly silent. When he spoke all gentleness was gone from his voice. "What the hell did you expect? Did you think you were going to let a tame tiger out of that stinking cage? Do you know he killed the guard that let him out with a crowbar before he went over the wall? He's been in there ten years and he's hardly human anymore."

"Are you?"

"I don't know. Maybe not. Maybe I'll end up doing exactly what he tried to do. If I have to ride much farther with you this close to me. . . ." He broke off and cursed savagely under his breath.

They reached the cut in the nearest hills, hills which were bleak piles of naked rock upon which nothing grew. Riding into that cut was like riding into an oven. Even the light breeze that had stirred the furnace air of the desert was still.

Donna felt her head reeling. She grasped the saddle horn and held on. She wondered if she was going to die before they reached their destination, and suddenly found she didn't care. Nothing lay ahead of her but the bitterness of vengeance. Nothing but degradation and misery. The blood that Varra would let must be on her hands as much as his.

She remembered something her father had once said . . . before he was hanged. "You can't touch dirt without getting it on your hands." She hadn't understood, then, that he was talking about people, but she understood it now. Varra was dirt and she had touched him and now she was dirty too.

Suddenly her self control snapped. She began to laugh hysterically. She screamed at the brassy sky, at the implacable, burning sun. The arm of Sands, around her waist, tightened involuntarily.

Varra swung his head. His eyes were yellow ice. "Shut that damned bitch up!"

Sands' voice was clipped with anger. "What do you expect from her? This is a decent woman. She risked her neck and put up the money to get you out. Don't you feel any gratitude at all?"

"Gratitude? Hell no! She didn't do it for me. She did it because she knew what I'd do the minute I got out of there. She wants somebody killed, Sands, and she knows I'm the only man that can do it."

Donna tried to stop the screaming laughter coming from her lips and failed. But it stopped being laughter, suddenly, and became weeping, bitter, lost, without restraint.

Sands stopped his horse. He said, "Go on ahead. I'll catch up with you."

Varra began to laugh. The sound was ugly and suggestive. Sands' voice was like a whip. "Shut up!"

Varra's laugh died out. He stared at Sands furiously for several moments as though wondering why he took orders from him. Then he touched his horse's sides with his heels and went on.

Sands pulled his horse into the shade of a towering rock face and swung to the ground. He put up his hands and lifted Donna down. She had stopped weeping but occasionally a sob broke from her throat.

She wouldn't look at him. He said softly, "I'm not going to touch you so you needn't be afraid."

She whispered, "I am afraid. He's only waiting until. . . ."

He said, "I won't let him."

"Why? What do you care what happens to me? You're free. That's what you wanted, isn't it?"

He nodded. "It's what I wanted." There was reserve in his voice as though he resented her implication that he was no better than Varra was.

She stared up into his face. There was hardness apparent in it and she guessed his eyes could be cold as ice. Yet the cruelty so apparent in Varra's face did not show in Sands'. She asked suddenly, "Why were *you* sent to Yuma?"

"Murder."

"Did you do it?"

"I did it. Now mount up and we'll go on."

She put her foot in the stirrup and swung to the saddle. He mounted behind her. The horse plodded away in the tracks left by Varra's horse and the pack animal only moments before.

Chapter Six

At noon they stopped briefly, and each drank half a cup of water from one of the barrels lashed to the pack. Owen gave each of the horses a little water out of a canvas "morral", also carried on the pack. Donna didn't speak to either of the men. What talk there was between Sands and Varra was curt.

They went on afterward, and in mid-afternoon rode their exhausted horses into the yard of a small ranch nestled beside a damp place in the gulch.

There was a well beside the house. Varra went to it at once, pulled up the bucket and took a long drink while water streamed down and soaked his chest. He dropped the bucket back in and Sands pulled it up again. He gave it to Donna and she drank thirstily. He took it last, drank, and poured what was left on the top of his head.

A man came out of the house, a dried-up man with thinning, graying hair, carrying a rifle in his hand. Varra said, "We want to swap horses, mister. How much?"

The man walked into the yard warily. He went from one to another of the horses, critically inspecting them. At last he said shortly, "Hundred dollars a head."

"The hell! We'll give you twenty."

The man backed toward the house. "I know you're from Yuma. Now get the hell out of here. I could kill you and they'd give me fifty dollars a head for *you*."

Varra walked casually toward him. His voice was wheedling. "Listen, mister, we ain't millionaires. Twenty's a good price for swappin' them Injun ponies you got in your corral. Tell you what. I'll make it twenty-five."

"Get out of here."

The man started to raise his rifle but Varra was faster. He lunged at the man and batted the rifle barrel aside just as it discharged. He closed with the man and wrenched the rifle from his hands.

He started to swing around, knowing apparently that Sands constituted the greater threat. The rancher grappled with him, trying to recover the gun.

Varra swung the barrel and it connected with the side of the man's head. The rancher sagged, staggered a few steps and fell on his face. Sands said sharply, "Drop it!"

Varra froze. Slowly his head turned until he could look at Sands, who stood dripping fifteen feet away, his rifle centered on Varra's chest. Varra let the rifle slide out of his hands.

Sands said, "Step away from it."

Varra did, scowling. Sands told Donna to go pick it up and she did, taking care not to get within Varra's reach.

Inside the house, a woman screamed. She came running out, glanced at Varra and at Sands and then at her husband on the ground.

She was a withered, middle-aged woman with

soapsuds on her bare arms. The front of her dress was wet and also held flecks of suds.

She ran to her husband and flung herself down beside him. Sands said, "He's all right, ma'am. He'll have a headache is all." He glanced at Donna. "Give her seventy-five dollars. We'll get the horses."

Varra was still glowering at Sands, who said, "Bring your horse. We'll catch the best three in there and go."

Sullenly Varra picked up the reins of his horse. Owen followed, leading the other two. He turned his head and said as an afterthought, "Give her another seventy-five. We'll take four horses and leave our three."

The woman was kneeling dumbly beside her husband. Donna said, "I'll help you get him in."

The woman looked up. "What kind of woman are you, anyway, traveling with a pair like that . . . ?"

Donna wanted to tell her that except for Sands her husband would be dead. But she remained silent as she helped the woman drag her husband inside the house.

Varra had killed a prison guard. He would have killed this man. And how many more times, before they reached the Colorado high country, would he take a life?

She shuddered involuntarily. Guilt for each of Varra's killings must rest equally with her, she realized, for it was she who had obtained his release. And it was too late for going back.

The woman was down on the floor beside her husband, bathing his face and the bloody lump on his head with a wet cloth. Donna withdrew the heavy money sack from beneath her skirt. She counted out a hundred and fifty dollars and laid it on the table. She hesitated for a moment, wanting desperately to leave more. Then, firming her lips, she restored the sack to its place beneath her skirt. She crossed the room to another table, found pencil and paper, and scrawled out a bill of sale.

She didn't look at the woman again, but went outside. Varra and Sands had four of the corraled horses caught. They were busily changing saddles from the worn-out horses to the fresh ones. When they had finished, Sands led the packhorse over to the well, hauled up the bucket and began to refill the water casks. When he had finished he said shortly to Donna, "Mount up."

"You're not going to leave like this? Aren't you going to wait and see if he's all right?"

"No time. Anyhow, he'll be all right." He swung to the bareback horse, rode to the corral and opened the gate. He rode in and drove the remaining horses out. They galloped away except for the three worn-out ones, who stopped at the edge of the yard and stood there, heads hanging listlessly.

Varra had mounted, but he was staring speculatively at the shack. Owen said, "Come on, come on!" He rode to the packhorse and caught up his reins.

He rode out and Donna followed. Varra trailed the

pair reluctantly a hundred yards behind, looking back as though thinking of the rancher's rifle which Donna had left in the shack.

Donna stared steadily at Sands, riding ahead of her. He had saved the man's life at the risk of his own. Yet he had refused to be concerned about the still unconscious man.

What kind of man was he, she asked herself. She came up with no answers that satisfied her. He had admitted being a murderer, yet there was not the savagery in him that there was in Varra. Certainly he wasn't afraid of Varra though. . . .

Without turning his head, he called, "We ought to be all right now. We've got fresh horses and they haven't."

In the afternoon, the heat was unbearable. Donna's body was soaked. Little rivulets ran down her cheeks from her forehead. Dust rose from the hoofs of Sands' horse and from those of the pack animal he trailed behind.

A kind of hopeless lethargy possessed her and a strange certainty began to grow in her. She wasn't going to see the high country again. Death was riding with them through this furnace heat, waiting.

She turned her head and glanced at Varra. He was a tall man, and thin. She guessed his age at somewhere between thirty and forty.

His hat was pulled low over his eyes, concealing them. But she remembered them, close-set, almost yellow in color like the eyes of a mountain lion. She

could see his mouth, the lips cracked and full, surrounded by the thickness of his beard.

Unless you looked at his eyes, she thought, Varra
might be just another man. There was nothing particularly evil about him unless you saw his eyes.

But if you did . . . you understood what he was. A
man without conscience, untroubled by any feeling of
guilt over the things he did. Killing a man, or woman
would mean nothing at all to him. He would unthinkingly have killed both the man and woman back there
if he'd had a gun. And this was the monster she had
loosed upon the land. She turned her head and looked
at the rifle Sands carried loosely at his side. She
wished she had it now. She would raise it and kill
Varra with no regrets.

But she didn't have the rifle. She doubted if she
could get it from Sands even if she tried. She would
have to bide her time and watch and wait. The time
would come.

She stared broodingly at Sands' broad, muscular
back, to which his shirt was stuck with sweat. She
stared between him at the shimmering heat trapped
between the bare rock canyon walls. They were
climbing steadily. She wondered how long it would
be before they rode out of this murderous heat. Several days at least. Several days if they lived that long.

Toward evening, Sands stopped in the shade of one
of the canyon walls. He swung to the ground, hesitated a moment, then handed the rifle up to Donna.
He began to water the horses sparingly with the

60

canvas morral. Varra didn't even dismount. He sat his horse as though almost asleep. His eyes were half open and when they touched her, she felt a chill. She thought of the promise she'd made to herself a while ago but she didn't move. It wasn't in her to kill Varra in cold blood. No matter what he was.

She thought again of home. Home, for Donna, was a stout log ranchhouse lying at the head of an enormous green meadow through which a tumbling stream wound. A meadow that in fall was dotted with brown stacks of mountain hay, that in winter was covered with a white blanket of snow whose only flaws were the tracks of game and cattle criss-crossing it.

Behind the house, rising in a long, gentle grade to the jagged peaks of the Continental Divide, was T Diamond's rangeland, almost black with heavy spruce and pine, green in spots where groves of quaking aspen stood. Fall turned those patches flaming gold, spring made them a soft, light green.

At first snowfall, the cattle came trailing out of that high, lush summer range to gather in the meadow below the house . . . She felt a sharp nostalgia, nostalgia that turned bitter when she remembered her father was gone.

He was dead. They had hanged him from the hoist in the loft of his own hay barn, and left him for Donna to find. She'd had to climb up and cut him down. She'd had to dig his grave, and drag him to it because she couldn't lift him, and bury him.

Why? It all went back a long, long time, that bitterness which had brought about his death.

T Diamond had been only a shack in the high mountain country when it all began. The town of Cutbank had been a handful of similar shacks. The Radek place was a sod shanty in the cedar hills west of town.

Her mother had been stranded in Cutbank when the operator of a traveling show ran off and left her there. Donna had never known her, but she had seen a picture of her and knew how beautiful she had been.

Both Dan Radek and her father wanted the stranded girl. Even after her father and mother were married, Radek never gave up. He didn't give up even after Donna was born.

Nor had life in the high country, in that small log shack, been satisfying for the stranded girl. Radek had started coming by when her father was away and her mother had not discouraged him.

It ended as such things always end. Her father came home unexpectedly. . . .

The fight between them must have been a ferocious one, she thought. Because it had left them both unconscious in front of the small log shack. Her terrified and conscience-stricken mother had started for town with her. . . .

But a blizzard struck before she reached the town. She froze to death. But by covering her blanket-wrapped child with her own body she managed to keep Donna alive.

Both men lived, and each blamed the other for her

mother's death. Out of that grew the hatred that mounted with the years.

Radek had sons by the woman he married after that. He had five of them. Her father never re-married.

The drowsing violence erupted only recently and grew out of a simple thing as violence usually does. Donna thoughtlessly danced with Lee Radek, one of Dan's sons, at a town dance. Next morning Lee Radek was found dead halfway home from town.

Blinded by hatred and grief, Dan Radek swore her father had murdered Lee. He came up into the mountains with his sons at his back.

She could imagine what had happened then—the bitter quarrel, ending in a fight. And the hanging after her father had been subdued.

If she'd only been home, she thought. She might have prevented it. She'd have told them her father had been with her at the time Lee had to have been killed. But she hadn't been home. And her father was dead.

She remembered the hopelessness, the helplessness, the exhaustion that had followed the burial. For two days she sat in the house, staring emptily out the window. Until her hatred began to crystallize.

She went to Cutbank then. She swore out a warrant for their arrest. She stayed in town until they went to trial.

The trial had been a farce. She couldn't testify that she had seen them kill her father. She had read their tracks but the tracks were gone and had been seen by no one else. The Radeks claimed to have been in Cut-bank all night. The hotel clerk swore they had been at the hotel.

They were acquitted, and Donna went home alone. Not to forget. To brood, and plan.

Only one man, she learned, hated the Radek clan as she hated them. Max Varra was his name. They had used Varra cynically—to kill a neighbor whose land they wanted. They had brought him in and had paid him two hundred and fifty dollars for the killing. When it was done, they presented the sheriff with an airtight case. Tracks. One of Varra's spurs. An eye-witness who had seen Varra ride away from the neighbor's house, another who had heard Varra threaten him.

The trial was cut and dried. Only the fact that there was no eyewitness to the actual killing saved Varra's life. His attempt to implicate the Radeks failed. He got twenty years to life.

Varra didn't need to be told what he had to do now that he was free. He'd promised the Radeks death on the last day of his trial. And he'd get them now, one by one. He'd get them and Donna would get her revenge. If, she thought bleakly, Varra didn't kill her first.

Chapter Seven

The sun sank behind the hills and the soft beauty of the desert sunset gently stained the land, tempering its harshness and modifying its cruelty. They halted in first dusk and Sands built a fire. Varra watched impassively while Donna cooked supper over it.

He ate greedily, continuing to watch her steadily. She refused to meet his eyes. A feeling of coldness seeped through her, for she knew what he was thinking and what he would do if he could.

He would kill Sands, she thought. And with Sands gone . . . she might as well be dead too.

Sands scattered the fire's ashes when they were through eating. He said, "We'll go on in a couple of hours. You can sleep if you want to, ma'am."

She didn't move. He said, "You'll be all right. I'll stay awake."

Varra said mockingly, "Yeah. You lie down, ma'am. I'll come with you to make sure you don't get cold."

Sands said evenly, "You stay where you are."

Donna was trembling. She could scarcely see their faces—not well enough to tell what expressions they held.

Varra edged toward Sands. She glanced at Sands. The revolver was in his hands and the hammer made a soft click as he thumbed it back. Varra growled, "Put the gun away." His voice took on a wheedling tone like the one he'd used back there where they'd gotten horses earlier today. "You an' me don't want to be fightin' all the time. Not over a piece like that. She's only a woman, man. What the hell. . . ."

He was edging slowly toward Sands' horse. The rifle lay on the ground beside the horse. Sands said, "Stay put, Max. You go ahead and sleep, ma'am."

Varra spoke with mock regret as he reached the horse. "I guess I'm going to have to kill you after all."

"Now's a real good time to try."

Varra stooped and seized the rifle. He straightened.

Sands said, "Let it slide out of your hands, Max. Kick it toward me. Don't make any mistakes."

Varra froze. His body tense, he waited for a long, long time. Sands prodded, "I won't wait much longer. Drop it or use it. Now!"

For an instant, Donna thought Varra would. She held her breath and prayed softly that if he tried, Sands would kill him before he could. The moment, tense and brittle, dragged on until Donna thought she couldn't stand it any more. Then, abruptly, the rifle thumped on the ground. It skidded away from Varra as he kicked it free. Sands said, "Now back away."

Varra stood there defiantly for several moments. Then, as Sands approached, he backed away.

Sands waited until he was several steps away. He stooped to recover the gun.

Varra kicked. Sand showered Owen. But he got the rifle and straightened, stopping Varra's rush with a bullet blasted into the ground at Varra's feet. His voice was like a whip. "Next one's going in your guts!"

Varra stopped. Sands walked to Donna and handed her the rifle. "Use it on him any time you want." There was a certain self-disgust apparent in his voice. She realized that he had deliberately let Varra reach the rifle, intending to kill him when he did. Only he hadn't been able to when the time for it came.

The cold barrel and stock in her hands gave her a comforting feeling of security. Perhaps it was only a delusion, but for a moment it almost seemed to her that they might make it safely home.

She walked away from the ashes of the dead fire. She went beyond the horses. Changing directions then, she continued silently for about a hundred yards. She laid down in a small hollow. She put the rifle on the ground, then rolled until her body covered it. She rested her head on her arms, folded above her head.

She closed her eyes. The world seemed to reel when she did. She'd had no sleep last night and none today. She wondered if she could stay awake even if she wanted to.

Scarcely had she completed the thought when she fell asleep. She awakened to Sands' voice shouting, "Hey! It's time to go!"

She got to her feet and stumbled toward his voice. She blundered into the side of one of the horses, mounted and rested the gun across the saddle in front of her.

The horse moved out without urging. Again Sands

led, trailing the packhorse. Donna came second and Varra brought up the rear.

She tried to force the sleepiness from her mind. If she didn't stay on guard, Varra could range alongside before she realized it. He could snatch the rifle and shoot Sands in the back.

The worst of it was, she thought, that Varra could sleep in the saddle, sleep whenever there was opportunity for it. He would grow progressively more rested while she and Sands grew more tired. Eventually the time would come when neither of them could stay awake. That was the time Varra was waiting for.

The horses plodded ever north and the hours of night wore slowly away. She drowsed sometimes, and awoke each time with a nervous start. She found herself thinking of home without particular enthusiasm.

It was an empty place now, with ugly memories that would never fade. She would sell it, she thought, and go away.

Yet the thought of leaving was no more attractive than the thought of staying on.

The horses kept climbing steadily, and the early morning air was cool. Dawn came, lightening the sky slowly. Eventually the sun came up.

There was vegetation on these higher hills through which they rode. Cactus. Several kinds of brush and a little grass. And there was game. A deer came out of a thick clump of brush and stared at them.

Owen dropped back and said softly, "The rifle. Give it to me."

She handed it to him silently. He threw it to his shoulder and fired just as the deer began to move.

The animal dropped and lay still. Sands said, "Varra. Get over there and gut it out."

"You gut it out."

Donna glanced at him. Until now, she had seen no particular emotion in Varra, except when he looked at her. Now she saw hatred in his eyes, the intensity of which was startling. He *would* kill Sands, first chance he got.

Sands jacked another cartridge into the gun. He raised it to his shoulder and aimed carefully. He said, "If I put a bullet in your arm . . . you'd live, all right, but you wouldn't be threatening anybody for a while. Get off and gut that deer."

Varra got off his horse. He fished in his pocket for his knife, crossed the ravine to the deer, knelt and got to work. Sands turned his head toward her. There was something strange in his eyes. Pity perhaps. Or understanding. He said, "Know how far the next place where we change horses is?"

She frowned slightly, trying to remember. "I think . . . I don't know. I haven't been thinking of that. Maybe as we ride I'll remember. It must have been about a hundred miles from the other place. How far do you think we've come?"

"We haven't come that far. Let me know when you recognize landmarks."

Varra had finished with the deer. Sands trailed the packhorse across the gulch to where it lay. Varra lifted it on and tied it down. Both men returned and they formed a single file again. There was a road of sorts through here, though it was obviously a seldom traveled one. There were no tracks in it fresher than about three days and they were the tracks of unshod horses that might have been running loose.

As the sun rose, the heat increased. No small breeze stirred. Donna ached in every muscle. She had to force herself to remember the way her father had looked hanging in the barn to keep her hate alive.

She had seen people who lived with hate. She knew what it could do to her. She told herself she didn't care.

But riding along that day, her eyes rested more and more on the broad, strong back of Owen Sands ahead. She had brought him into it, and he would be a part of it.

Better, perhaps, if both of them died here in the bleak, scorching Arizona mountains. Because if they went on, only tragedy could result. For themselves and for the people of the country where she had been born.

Chapter Eight

Today, Owen Sands kept Varra riding in the lead. That way, he could watch the man and there would be no chance of Varra surprising Donna and getting her gun from her. The day wore on, and in late afternoon puffy clouds began to fill the sky until at last they covered it and obscured the sun.

Memories crowded his mind, memories of his trial, of the long ride to Yuma, manacled like some wild thing, of the first horrible months of his confinement there.

A convicted murderer. An escaped convict. He was both these things and would be hunted like an animal the rest of his life. No matter where he went or what he did, no matter how long a time elapsed, he would always wonder when a hand would fall on his shoulder or when a lawman's gun would nudge him in the back.

Nor was there any way of changing it. He had killed the man he had been convicted of murdering. If he hadn't been able to prove it was self-defense at his trial, he'd not be able to prove it now.

But it had been self-defense. James Trask had a gun in his hand when Owen shot. Someone had taken the gun out of his hand after he was dead. Or picked it up nearby. It had probably been one of Trask's brothers or his father. Owen's mistake had been in leaving the scene to go after the doctor. It had been a mistake to leave the scene at all.

He'd paid enough for that mistake. His jaw tightened grimly. He'd pay no more. No matter what, they'd never get him into Yuma Prison again. He'd make them kill him first.

Behind him, Donna said, "That mountain there . . . I recognize it. The ranch where we change horses is right at the foot of it."

Owen turned his head, then followed the direction she was pointing with his glance. The mountain she referred to was twenty miles away. They ought to reach it about an hour after dark.

Owen closed his eyes. His head dropped forward and he felt sleep clutching at his mind. He jerked himself awake and glanced at Varra up ahead.

Even if he could prove now that Trask had had a gun, it wouldn't help. Varra had killed the guard. Both he and Varra were equally guilty of that killing under the law. And properly so, Sands thought. He hadn't even tried to stop Varra from killing El Azote. He'd been too intent on his own escape.

Yet even being hunted for the rest of his life was better than staying in Yuma. Anything, even death, was preferable to that.

He caught himself dozing again, and yanked himself awake a second time. This time he caught Varra staring back at him, a mocking, triumphant expression on his face. Varra had been sleeping in the saddle all day. He was rested and wide awake. He was waiting, patiently, for his chance.

Mile after mile passed beneath their horses' hoofs.

Light began to fade from the cloudy sky. At last it turned completely dark.

Varra's shape ahead was now only a darker blur against the blackness of the land. Sands occasionally shook his head savagely to stay awake. He could hear the sounds made by Donna's horse behind.

No use stopping to rest the horses now, he thought. Soon they'd have fresh animals. He began to study the land ahead, and once veered slightly to the right when Donna called, "We're too far to the left."

He saw the light at last, flickering faintly through the night. A dog began to bark. Another light appeared as a door was opened. A man stood in the doorway, a rifle in his hand.

Varra rode to within a dozen yards of the door before he stopped. Sands halted his horse a little behind him. He said, "Howdy. We need fresh horses. Want to make a trade?"

The man stepped back into the house. He reappeared a moment later with a lantern in his hand. He still held the rifle in the other and he stared up at the trio warily.

"Might. How bad you want to trade?" He walked past Sands and stared up at Donna. He inspected the horses, one by one. Then he turned and said, "Yuma?"

Sands realized his ankle was showing, the manacle marks plain on it. He said, "Never mind. We want horses and we're willing to pay for 'em."

"Fifty dollars a head."

Owen turned his horse. "Come on, Varra. We don't need horses that bad."

The man said "Twenty-five?"

Owen turned back. "Let's take a look at what you got."

"Corral's this way." The man walked away into the darkness.

Owen followed, after first dropping back and taking the rifle out of Donna's hands. He stayed just behind Varra and, even when they reached the corral, did not get closer to him than a dozen feet. He said, "Go in and pick out four, Varra."

Varra followed the man into the corral. The two of them selected four horses, caught them and tied them to the fence. The man came out and led the others in. He and Varra began to switch saddles and packs. When they were finished, the man came out and looked at Sands. "Four at twenty-five each is a hundred. Twenty-five extra if you want a saddle for that barebacked horse."

Sands said, "Give it to him, Miss Tate."

He heard the clink of coins as she counted out the gold. Sands took the beat-up saddle the man gave him and tossed it on the barebacked horse. He mounted and said, "Lead out, Varra. We'll turn west here."

Varra glanced at him quickly, but said nothing. He led out of the yard, heading west. Sands watched the man with the lantern until they were out of rifle range. When the light was only a speck in the night, he said, "You can turn north now."

Varra did. Sands dropped back and returned the rifle to Donna. He wondered if he could stay awake tonight. If he couldn't. . . .

They traveled steadily until midnight. The land began to rise after they left the ranch house. It stretched away ahead in rising ridges that ended in the distant, snow-covered peaks Sands had glimpsed the day before. Somewhere up there was Colorado, and Donna's home.

He halted at last beside a narrow stream. He swung down stiffly, feeling the chill of the night air, feeling his weariness like a drug.

Varra flopped to the ground, holding his horse's reins. Sands paced back and forth, afraid to lie down, afraid to rest. If he ever closed his eyes he'd sleep as though he were dead.

Talk would help, he supposed. He glanced toward Donna and said, "You'll be home soon. What happens then?"

She did not reply.

Sands persisted, "Varra said something about you wanting a man killed. Who?"

"Dan Radek."

"Why? What'd he do to you?"

For a long time she was silent. When her voice finally came through the darkness it was tight, angry and charged with hatred. "Because he hanged my father. I found him—hanging from the hoist on the barn. I cut him down. . . ." He heard her breath draw in, long and shuddering. For several moments afterward her teeth chattered helplessly.

"I dug his grave. I had to drag him to it and roll him in. . . ."

He said, "Haven't you got any law up there? Couldn't you go to the law?"

She laughed shortly, bitterly. "Law! I went to it. But by the time the sheriff got there all the tracks were gone. Radek swore he had been in town and bought witnesses to back him up. They acquitted him."

"How does Varra come into it?"

"He hates Radek and his sons as much as I do— maybe more. They hired him for a killing and then fixed it so he would be convicted of it. They sent him to Yuma and he won't rest until he's paid them back."

Sands resumed his pacing almost frantically. He felt as though he could go to sleep on his feet. Donna watched him for several moments, then said, "I've been dozing in the saddle all day. I can stay awake if you'd like to get a little sleep."

He started to say no, but stopped himself. He nodded reluctantly. He did need sleep. She could waken him if Varra tried anything. He flopped to the ground and closed his eyes. He murmured sleepily, "If he moves . . . if he comes this way . . . don't wait. Wake me."

She did not reply, or if she did, he didn't hear it. He slept as though he were dead.

It was a drugged and dreamless sleep at first. Later he dreamed—of the pit at Yuma, of the stench and nearly unbreathable air. The welts on his back put there by El Azote's whip burned like fire. His head ached from the savage blow of the length of chain.

He dreamed that Varra was creeping up on him. There was a scuffle. . . .

He wakened with a start, hearing immediately the sounds of a scuffle nearby. Still numb from sleep, he struggled to his feet, his hand going instantly to his waist where the revolver was.

It was still there, at least. He lunged toward the sounds just as Donna cried out with pain. He saw the two scuffling figures separate and saw Varra whirl, the rifle in his hands.

He reached the man before the rifle could bear. He batted the muzzle aside. . . .

Varra was on him like a tiger, using the rifle butt. It struck one of Sands' shoulders and turned it numb. Sands backed and as Varra lunged at him again, got both hands on the rifle.

Straining, grunting, heaving, the two fought for possession of it.

And Varra cursed—in a steady stream—the vicious, unspeakable obscenities of the prison. His breath came in short gasps, but each gasp carried a curse.

They fell beneath one of the horse's hoofs and the animal danced away nervously. Neither relinquished his grip on the rifle. Varra's knee came up. . .

And suddenly fury drove the remaining numbness of sleep from Owen's mind. He wrenched savagely at the gun and it tore out of Varra's grasp. Before the man could move he brought it around in a short, vicious arc and caught Varra on the side of the head with its stock.

The man collapsed. Sands struggled to his feet. He stood over Varra for several long moments, his breath dragging painfully into his starving lungs, expelling as painfully. Donna was weeping hysterically.

He walked to where she was huddled on the ground. He said harshly, "Get up. You let him out of his cage, and it's too late to change it now."

Her weeping subsided to a kind of hopeless whimpering. He repeated, more harshly than before, "Get up and take his gun. Next time he tries that, kill him."

She got up, without help from Sands. He thrust the rifle at her and she took it. He turned, caught his horse and the packhorse, then swung to the saddle, holding the packhorse's reins. "Come on. He'll follow when he comes to."

She mounted and followed him silently. He rode out, north, leaving Varra on the ground and Varra's horse tied to a clump of brush nearby.

From now on, he'd tie Varra to a tree every time they stopped. At least that way he could get some sleep.

Gray finally lightened the eastern sky. The sun rose, staining the sky a brilliant red. The peaks ahead were clearer today, snow visible on their barren crests.

What would he do, Sands wondered, when their destination was reached. Lose himself, he supposed. Find a mining camp somewhere, or an isolated ranch. Maybe he'd go to Canada.

He owed it to this girl, though, to see her safely home. She hadn't intended to buy him out of Yuma, but she had done it anyway. Without her, he would still have been inside.

He asked suddenly, "Why did Radek hang your father?"

At first he thought she hadn't heard. He was about to repeat his question when she said, "Radek thought father had killed one of his sons. I . . . I guess it was my fault in a way. I danced with Lee Radek and he was killed on his way home from the dance. They thought my father had done it, but he hadn't. I was with him at the time Lee Radek was killed."

He turned his head and looked at her pale, drawn face. There had to be more, he thought. There had to be a foundation of hatred to make the Radeks believe her father capable of killing one of them just for dancing with her. But he didn't question her further because he could see how painful were her memories.

In mid-morning he heard Varra coming up behind. He halted and waited until Varra caught up. The man looked at him with smoldering hatred, but he didn't speak.

Varra would kill him, he thought, the first time he got the chance. Killing was Varra's answer to everything. Frowning, he motioned Varra to take the lead and followed him warily through the scattered pines.

Chapter Nine

This night, they camped in a stand of heavy pines. Less than a hundred feet away a stream made a steady, unchanging roar. Owen cut some pieces of meat off the carcass of the deer and tossed them in a pan. Varra gathered wood and built a fire. Donna knelt beside it and began to cook the meat and to boil coffee. Owen unsaddled the horses and picketed them.

When the meal was ready, Owen took his plate and coffee cup away from the fire and sat down on a fallen log. He ate hungrily, then rolled a smoke with tobacco and papers which Donna had been thoughtful enough to include with her supplies. He rested there lazily, staring through the darkness toward the fire.

The smell of pine smoke was in his nostrils along with the wild, free smell of the pine woods. The sound of the stream was in his ears, and occasionally the raucous squawking of a jay.

He'd never thought he'd breathe this kind of air again. He'd never thought he'd smell campfire smoke or feel a horse between his knees. Even if he was caught, he'd have had this much.

Varra watched Donna steadily. A painful flush mounted in her face. Sands said impatiently, "Varra! Get up and come over here."

The man got up. Owen said, "Get me some of the rope lashings off the pack."

"What the hell do you think you're goin' to do?"

"Tie you up for the night. I need some sleep. Tonight I'm going to get some in spite of you."

"Like hell!"

Owen said harshly, "You choose, mister. You choose right now. If you want trouble then go ahead and give me an argument." He moved toward Varra.

The man backed from him, glancing around for a weapon. Sands said, "I'm not going to fight you again, so don't bother. Either go over and sit down with your back to that tree or I'll shoot you down. Make up your mind and make it up now."

"You won't shoot me. That damned woman needs me and you know she does."

"But I don't. I don't need you at all."

Varra stared at him a moment. Suddenly he stooped and seized a short, heavy branch he had previously gathered for firewood.

Sands raised the revolver and thumbed the hammer back. He sighted carefully and began deliberately to squeeze off his shot.

Varra yelled, "All right!" He dropped the branch. Sullenly he went over to the tree Sands had indicated and sat down, putting his back to it.

Sands released the hammer and thrust the gun into his belt. He took a length of rope from Donna, who had watched with white-faced fright. He said, "Stand to one side. Cock that rifle and if he makes a move, shoot him."

She nodded wordlessly. Sands made a loop in the end of the rope. Kneeling, he slipped it over Varra's feet, staying far enough back so the man couldn't kick out at him. Holding the slack end, he rose.

He put his foot on Varra's legs and tightened the loop. Moving behind the tree, he pulled in slack until Varra's feet were tight against his rump.

He began to walk around the tree, pulling the rope

tight each time he did. When Varra was securely trussed, he brought the rope around and, without fear this time, again looped it around Varra's ankles.

With the end, he tied Varra's hands together, tightening the rope cruelly until Varra began to curse. He said mildly, "I can stuff something in your mouth if you insist."

"You son-of-a-bitch!"

Sands cuffed him across the mouth. A thin trickle of blood came from one corner of it. Sands said, "Never mind. I know it by heart. You'll kill me. Wasn't that what you were about to say?"

Varra didn't speak, but his eyes were virulent.

Sands worked a few moments more, checking his knots, checking the lashings for slack. Satisfied, he returned to the fire. He dragged his saddle over close to it and laid down, his head on the saddle.

He closed his eyes. And almost instantly he slept.

It was a dreamless sleep tonight, a heavy sleep from which he did not awaken until the sky was gray with dawn. The first sounds he heard were those made by Varra, sullenly cursing.

He got up, stretched and began to gather wood for a fire. Donna awakened, got up and began to help. When he had the fire going, Sands crossed to Varra and untied him. Varra struggled to his feet with difficulty, took a step and fell. Cursing, he fought his way up a second time.

Sands stared at him without pity. Varra began to pace back and forth stiffly beside the fire, trying to restore circulation to his legs. He rubbed his wrists angrily, one after the other.

While Donna prepared fried meat and coffee for breakfast, Sands saddled the horses and put the pack on the packhorse. The three ate in almost sullen silence.

With the fire killed, the cooking utensils put away and the pack lashed down, they mounted and rode north again. The sun rose and climbed slowly across the morning sky.

Varra still rode in the lead, with Sands behind him. Donna brought up the rear.

Sands felt rested for the first time since leaving the prison. He began to look ahead, to try and plan.

He had no idea where he'd go. He knew he'd be wise not to stay in the same locality with Varra. Varra was going to kill the Radek family. He'd bring the attention of the law down on him.

The miles dragged past. They climbed steadily all through the day until at nightfall they were just below the barren peaks of the divide. This night was cold, but in spite of it, Owen again lashed Varra to a tree.

The following day, and the day following that were much the same, except for the fact that they crossed the divide, descended on the other side, then climbed a second range.

Donna, recognizing landmarks, began to direct them. At last they topped a long, wooded ridge and could stare downward into a wide valley in which Donna had said her ranch buildings lay.

She left them immediately, galloping on ahead. Sands, sitting his horse a dozen yards from Varra, stared into the valley below, shadowed by the setting sun.

He could see what was left of the buildings. He could see the thin plume of smoke that still drifted up from one of them.

But there was nothing left. Nothing but charred log walls, a rubble of charred timbers and ashes within the walls. Even the corral had been destroyed.

He motioned for Varra to go ahead, then picked his way down the slope after him. The two reached the bottom and crossed the valley floor.

A stream wound through the meadow, passing within a hundred yards of the burned buildings. Owen halted his horse and let him drink. Then he spurred the animal and caught up with Varra.

Donna Tate was sitting on the ground, her face buried in her hands. She raised her glance, her eyes swimming with tears. Owen asked, "Radek?"

"It must have been. No one else would do a thing like this." She got up. She had the pouch in which she kept her money in her hands. She crossed to Varra and held it out to him. "Get them," she said. "Get every one of them."

Varra took the pouch without dismounting. Then he turned and rode down the valley. He did not look back. He disappeared into a fringe of pines at the valley's edge half a mile below the house.

For a long time, Owen Sands stared after him. Then

he turned his head and looked at the girl. Her face was streaked with tears. There was a dull, hopeless look in her eyes.

He glanced toward the burned-out buildings. There was nothing left here for her. There was not even shelter and she had given the last of her money to Varra.

He asked, "What are you going to do?"

"I don't know. I don't care." There was dullness in her voice, and hopelessness.

Owen knew he was a fool if he stayed. He was free. He could go wherever he pleased. He owed it to himself to avoid being caught and returned to Yuma if it was possible.

But he also knew he couldn't leave her here this way. With impatient, self-directed anger, he swung from his horse and began to gather wood for a fire.

While the blaze was growing, he unsaddled the horses and picketed them.

Donna got up with an obvious effort and began listlessly to cook some meat. Sands filled the coffee pot at the stream and brought it back.

He squatted on his heels and stared into the fire. The gray of the sky faded and a few scattered stars winked out.

Moving about, doing something, seemed to help her state of mind. She finished cooking the meat and brought a plate to him. She filled his coffee cup and when he met her eyes, managed a wan smile. "I guess I'm a fool, Mr. Sands. I've gone to all this trouble.

I've spent every cent I was able to raise. And now I don't seem to care whether he kills them or not. It doesn't seem to matter anymore."

"It's the let-down. You'll feel better tomorrow."

"What are you going to do? I suppose you'll be leaving tonight."

For several moments he didn't reply. He knew he should say yes. He should mount the horse and leave—before he got caught up in what would happen here—before he was captured and returned to Yuma. But instead he said, "I'll stick around a day or two. I'll help you throw up some kind of shack. Tomorrow I'll go to town and get some supplies. The packhorse will bring enough to keep you going a little while."

"I hadn't thought of that."

He made a cigarette and puffed it lazily. "What kind of men are they? The Radeks, I mean? Why did they burn you out?"

She shrugged.

"Do they hate you too?"

"I don't think so. I suppose Dan Radek couldn't stand to see these buildings here. They reminded him of her . . . of my mother I mean."

"Was he in love with her?"

"Both he and my father were. I thought I'd told you. They fought over her after my father discovered Dan Radek had been seeing her. While they fought, she left for Cutbank, taking me. She was caught in a storm on the way and died of the cold.

But she covered me with her body and kept me alive."

Sands stared into the fire. He could almost see the two men battling so savagely here on this spot. He could imagine the woman, fleeing in terror with her child in her arms. Each man had probably blamed the other for her death. And had hated all the more.

He got up. "We'd better get some sleep. Big day tomorrow."

"Yes. I suppose we should. I don't know whether I can sleep or not. I can't rebuild anything by myself. And there's no money left."

"You've still got the land. You can sell that."

She didn't reply. Owen got his blanket and laid down beside the fire. He closed his eyes, but he didn't sleep.

He felt trapped, and angry because he did. He owed Donna something because through her he had escaped from Yuma Prison. Yet how much did he owe her? Did he owe it to her to stay here until he was recaptured and sent back? Impatiently he shook his head.

Hatred and thirst for revenge had caused the trouble she was in. Nor was it finished yet. Varra would kill the Radeks—some of them at least. He was crafty and merciless and would not be easily caught. Donna might be tried for complicity. She might have to answer to the law, with Varra, for every murder he committed.

He slept at last, but it was not an easy sleep.

Through it Varra paraded, cursing, threatening. . . .

He awakened once during the night and instantly reached for his gun. His hand relaxed immediately.

The sound that had awakened him was that of a woman crying. It was a muffled sound, as though her face were buried in her arms.

He laid awake for a long time, listening. He felt pity for her but he knew he couldn't help. This was something she would have to settle with herself.

Chapter Ten

Sands was up before Donna awakened. He gathered wood for a fire quietly and started it. He paused a moment to stare down at her.

She looked helpless and small lying there. Her face was streaked with tears, her hair uncombed. She was shivering with the cold.

He piled more wood on the fire, then walked among the blackened ruins of the buildings that had so recently stood here. There were enough unburned boards, he decided, for a roof. He could build a small cabin out of logs. But he'd need an axe and a saw. He'd need some nails.

He crossed to the wreckage of the barn and picked his way through it. He found several sets of harness and dragged them out onto bare ground. He began trying to make one good set out of the unburned portions of several sets. He heard Donna call and turned his head. He rose and walked toward her.

"There's enough harness there to salvage one good set."

"Why do you need harness?"

"To skid logs. We'll have to use logs to build a cabin. There isn't enough lumber left."

"You're going to stay?"

He shrugged. "For a little while."

"Why? I'd think. . . ."

He said, "You didn't plan to get me out of Yuma but you did. I'm free and I owe that much to you. I'll stay at least until you get a roof over you."

She seemed confused. She picked up the coffee pot, carried it to the stream, filled it and brought it back. She put it on to heat. Owen returned to the pile of harness and worked steadily until she called him to eat.

He ate quickly, then saddled one horse and put the pack-saddle on another. He said, "I'll be back before long. I'd stay out of sight if I were you."

She nodded and Sands rode away, following the direction in which Varra had gone last night.

A road of sorts followed the edge of the meadow in a downstream direction for about a mile and a half below the burned buildings, then, where the meadow narrowed out, entered heavy timber and began a more precipitous descent.

Here, he supposed, was where Donna's mother had been caught by the storm, where she had died of cold. In spite of the trouble she had caused, he felt a touch of sympathy for her. She had obviously not been used to the harsh and lonely life out here.

But she had certainly stirred up one hell of a feud, he mused wryly, a feud that still endured twenty years after her death.

The road dropped steadily through heavy timber for about ten miles. There were no fresh tracks in the road except for those made last night by Varra's horse. He wondered idly where Varra was right now. Hating the way he did, the man wouldn't waste any time beginning his quest for revenge. He was probably on his way to the Radek place right now.

About four miles from town, the road was joined by another. At this point, Sands could see the plain, stretching away twenty miles to another mountain range, the town of Cutbank, nestling immediately below him on the near rim of the plain and the low, cedar covered hills that bordered Cutbank on the west.

He began the descent, which was even steeper than before, and shortly thereafter negotiated a series of switchbacks on a bare, brushy ridge to enter Cutbank by its main street which sloped steeply all the way to the center of town.

The upper part of town consisted of residences, all of them frame, most of them white. Where the street leveled out, the business houses began, lining the street on both sides.

There was a hotel, three stories high and liberally decorated with scrollwork at the eaves. There were three mercantile stores, a saddle shop, a gunsmith, two dressmaker's shops. There were four or five saloons and a poolhall. In the block immediately below the hotel a square stone building housed the sheriff's office and the jail. Beyond, facing each other across the dusty street were two livery barns.

Sands rode directly to the largest of the livery barns and swung down from his horse. He tied his saddle horse to the rail, then led the pack animal inside.

A man sitting on a bench mending harness looked up at him. "Howdy."

Owen said, "You buy horses?"

The man nodded, getting up. He walked around the horse, inspecting him. He stopped at the horse's head and took the horse's muzzle in both hands. He inspected the animal's teeth judiciously, then turned his head. "Got a bill of sale?"

Sands shook his head. "I traded for him a couple of hundred miles back. But I'll give you a bill of sale."

"Forty dollars. Five more if you want to let the packsaddle go."

Sands said, "Fifty for both."

"Done. There's paper and a pencil in the tackroom there. Write me out a bill of sale."

Owen glanced at the brand on the horse's hip. He went into the tackroom and wrote out a bill of sale. The man came in, took the paper and read it. He gave Owen two twenty dollar gold pieces and a ten. Owen said, "Thanks," and went outside.

He stood for a moment, staring up the street. Then, leading his horse, he walked toward one of the mercantile stores.

Passing the sheriff's office, he glanced down uneasily to be sure his trousers covered his scarred ankles, and decided that they did. He heard a door open, heard a deep voice say, "Howdy. Stranger, ain't you?"

He stopped, and turned. There was an empty feeling in his chest, a ball of ice in his stomach. This was the way it would always be, he thought, from now until he died. He nodded bleakly, and waited.

The man who had spoken was in his fifties, Owen guessed. He wore a long, cavalry-style mustache, but otherwise was clean-shaven. He was stocky and powerfully built and his face was like old saddle leather.

Sharp blue eyes peered out from beneath bushy, graying brows. The sheriff smiled and stuck out a hand. "I'm Will Purdy. If you're lookin' for a job, maybe I can put you onto one."

Sands took the hand warily. It was strong and friendly, nothing more. He said, "Maybe later. Not right now."

"Sell your packhorse to Schuyler?"

Owen grinned. "You don't miss much, do you?"

"Nope."

Owen thought bleakly that Purdy probably hadn't missed the brand on his saddle horse, either. That brand, he realized suddenly, would create a link between Varra and himself, a link between himself and Yuma prison. But probably not just yet. Varra wasn't fool enough to let himself be recognized.

Purdy, still grinning, asked, "What'd the old bandit give you for it, if you don't mind my asking you?"

"Fifty dollars. For the horse and the packsaddle both."

"Then you got eatin' money for a while. If you don't lose it in a poker game."

Owen stared at him. He asked suddenly, "You this nosy with everyone?"

The sheriff laughed. It was a deep, chuckling laugh that contained genuine amusement. "Come to think of it, I guess I am. If you decide you want a job, just let me know."

Sands nodded, turned and continued up the street. He could almost feel the sheriff watching him and it gave him a sensation of uneasiness.

This was the sheriff, he thought, who had arrested Dan Radek for the murder of Donna's father. And yet, he supposed it was unfair to blame Purdy for that miscarriage of justice. Donna herself had admitted that the tracks had been wiped out. Against perjured evidence in court there wasn't much Purdy could have done.

He reached the mercantile store and tied his horse. He glanced back as he went inside and saw that Purdy was still watching him.

He bought an axe and saw and a gunnysack half full of supplies. Coffee. Flour. Sugar. Beans. Some canned goods. Nails and a hammer. He bought a cheap pair of boots, not because he either wanted or needed them, but because they would cover the scars on his ankles. He bought a cartridge belt and holster for the gun, and a box of cartridges.

He paid for his purchases, and when the storekeeper went up front for change, hastily put on the boots. He tossed the shoes Donna had provided into the gunnysack.

He went out and tied the axe and saw on first. Then he tied on the gunnysack. He mounted and rode out of town. Glancing back, he saw that Purdy was out of sight.

Purdy was a garrulous man, he thought, but he was not a fool. As soon as he discovered Varra was here, and that Donna Tate was back . . . As soon as he discovered that Sands was staying at her place. . . . He'd put two and two together soon enough. He'd know Sands was also an escapee from Yuma. He'd take him into custody.

Sands' mouth tightened grimly. He wasn't going to wait for that. He wasn't going to stay that long. He ought to be able to put up some kind of cabin for Donna in a couple of days. Then he could leave.

His horse climbed steadily, negotiated the switchbacks and began to climb through the timber. At intervals, Sands halted him and let him blow. He reached the junction of the two roads without meeting anyone and took the turn toward Donna's place.

She was sitting on the ground when he arrived, busily assembling a set of harness from the partly burned sets he had earlier dragged out of the charred rubble of the barn. He halted and unloaded the horse. It was early afternoon, he judged.

He squatted and helped her with the harness until it was finished. Then, while she built up the fire and started preparing dinner, he harnessed her saddle horse.

He found a singletree that was not too badly burned, and a length of chain. Carrying the axe, leading the harnessed horse, he started up the hill behind the house.

He worked steadily, efficiently. Three trees crashed to the ground. He topped them, and trimmed them, then hooked the chain around the butt end of one and began snaking it down the hill.

Donna had dinner ready for him, so he stopped long enough to eat. She didn't speak, but watched him steadily as he did. He puzzled at the unreadable expression in her eyes. She was trying to figure him out, he decided finally. She was trying to understand him, and the crime for which he had been sentenced.

He looked at her suddenly, vaguely irritated in spite of himself. "What have you decided about me?"

She flushed uncomfortably, but did not evade his question nor pretend to misunderstand. She said in a small, uncertain voice, "I think someone must have made a mistake. I don't think you murdered anyone."

"I never said I did."

"But you said. . . ."

"I said I'd killed the man I was tried for killing. There's a difference. It was a fight. If I hadn't shot him, he'd have shot me. Only I was fool enough to go for the doctor afterward. When I got back, his gun had disappeared and he was dead. They convicted me of shooting an unarmed man."

She seemed visibly relieved. He could not resist saying, "But you don't know if I'm telling the truth or not, do you? There isn't a man in Yuma who doesn't swear he was innocent. Not many at least."

She said, not looking at him, "You kept Varra away from me. You're staying when you know it's dangerous, just to build a shelter for me."

Even more irritated than before, and not understanding why, he got suddenly to his feet. "If I don't get it done, I'll still be here when that talky sheriff comes after me."

"You've met the sheriff?"

"I met him. Or rather he met me." He left the fire and jumped to the harnessed horse's back. He rode up the hill, hooked onto another log and snaked it down.

All afternoon his axe rang steadily. One after another the tall pines crashed to the ground. When dusk made it impossible to continue, he had almost twenty logs lying at the bottom.

He ate silently and afterward rolled up wearily in his blankets. He stared at the fire for a long, long time. He found himself wishing he didn't have to leave. He liked it here. He liked the smell of pines, the clear, cold air, the sound of the narrow, rushing stream.

But there was no use thinking of that. In another

96

day or two, Varra would begin his executions of the Radek clan. And then all hell was going to break loose.

Chapter Eleven

The road between the Tate place and the town of Cutbank was a familiar one to Max Varra. He'd been over it several times when he had been here before.

The light faded steadily as he rode, and at last a few scattered stars winked out.

The Radeks were first, he thought. He'd kill them one by one, if possible letting each see him and know why before he died. But there was another score to settle later on. Before he left the country, he was going to kill Owen Sands.

He reached the fork in the road and paused briefly to stare into the black void, to stare at the dimly winking lights of the town below. Then, almost impatiently, he rode on.

A mile beyond the fork, he heard someone coming and pulled off the road to wait until they passed. His hand went forward and covered his horse's nostrils so that the animal wouldn't give him away.

A horse and rider passed, dimly visible but not recognizable in the darkness. When all sound had died away, Varra returned to the road and continued his descent.

He didn't dare be seen in town, he thought. Too many people were still here that would recognize him. But he had to have a gun and some supplies.

He reached the edge of town and rode slowly down the dark, tree-shaded street. When he reached the edge of the business district he turned right and entered the alley. He dismounted now and led his horse.

It was lucky, he thought, that he knew this town and remembered it. Delaney's Mercantile was down this way. It ought to be closed up for the night. He could get in the back way, get guns and ammunition and supplies and get out again. He could leave town and no one would even know he had been here.

He found himself thinking of the Radeks and a sudden wildness possessed him. Killing had been Max Varra's business for a long, long time, but it had been a business, one he carried out dispassionately and without feeling. The Radek clan was different. He was going to enjoy killing each one of them. He was going to savor the terror that would possess those remaining as one after another of their number was found dead.

He reached the rear of Delaney's store. The air was chill now, and a steady breeze blew down across town from the high peaks south of it. Max shivered slightly as his hands went out to feel the door. There was a hasp on the outside, but no padlock. The upper half of the door was glass. All he had to do was break the glass and reach inside. . . .

He picked up a rock and tapped the window lightly. It broke, making some noise but not very much. Carefully now, he picked the shards of glass out of the window frame, laying each one carefully at his feet.

When the window frame was free of broken glass, he reached in and slid the bolt that secured the door on the inside. But he did not go in. He waited for a long time, listening.

A lot of years had passed, while he rotted in Yuma. But not so many that he couldn't remember every detail of his arrest and trial. When they'd found him guilty. . . . His eyes gleamed fiercely in the darkness. He'd gone wild with rage, he remembered. He'd tried to kill Dan Radek right there in the courtroom with his hands.

He'd damn near succeeded too. It had taken five men to subdue him and get him off Radek, who was beginning to turn blue. It had been a fight all the way to the door, with the spectators crowding each other in terror trying to get away from it. But once outside, once out of the judge's sight, a well placed blow from the sheriff's revolver barrel had stopped his struggles and he hadn't remembered anything else until he woke up in his cell.

Maybe he'd get a chance at that damned sheriff before he left. But the Radeks came first. They were the ones responsible for all those years in Yuma, for all the things he had endured. They'd hired him for a killing and then had betrayed him and turned him in to the sheriff along with enough evidence to convict him and send him to prison for twenty years.

Quietly, he opened the door and stepped inside. He

stood still in the darkness for several moments, waiting until his eyes would become accustomed to it and trying to remember the layout of the store.

There ought to be an aisle through this back room leading to the front of the store. The guns and ammunition were on the right, about halfway to the door.

At least that was where they had been ten years ago. He began to move forward up the narrow aisle, feeling his way, careful not to stumble or make any unnecessary noise.

The guns were where he had expected them to be. By feel, he selected a repeating carbine and a revolver. He opened the ammunition drawer and still working by feel, by inserting cartridges into the weapons he had chosen, found the right calibers. Once he did, he took a box of each.

Now he moved across the store and toward the rear, where the grocery section was. He found a flour sack and dumped in a couple of dozen cans selected at random in the darkness. He found a sack of beans and dumped in several double handfuls, loose. He put his cartridges in on top. Hefting the sack and rifle, with the revolver stuffed into his belt, he returned to the back door and went outside.

He listened again, careful. Then he tied his sack of supplies on the saddle, mounted, rode to the end of the alley and stopped.

People were crossing this side street down at the end of the block. He heard the faint tinkle of a piano in one of the saloons. Somewhere a man laughed and a woman squealed. A dog began to bark.

He left the alley mouth, turning left. He continued along the side street until he left the last few scattered houses at the edge of town behind. Only then did he lift his horse to a steady, trotting gait.

He circled the town and found the road leading into the cedar-covered hills west of it. He let his horse drop back into a walk, thinking sourly that, if he were to succeed, he would have to force himself to be patient. He didn't want to be patient. He had waited ten years. Every day of those ten years he had killed Dan Radek in his thoughts. He had done it quickly with his gun; he had done it slowly the way an Indian would. Now, thinking of Dan Radek so close to him. . . .

Yet he realized that if revenge were to be thoroughly satisfying and complete, it would have to be carefully executed. No one must know he was in the country. And if anyone found out, they had to die before they could spread the word.

Radek's place was six or seven miles from town. The road followed a dry stream bed which carried no water from early spring until late fall. About four miles from town the valley widened out to about a mile.

A late-rising moon came up, bathing the valley with a cold, cheerless glow. Varra could see the dark shapes of cattle against the lighter background of the land.

He left the road now cautiously, continuing at a walk. He'd find a spot from which he could see the house. He'd watch, until he saw one of them leave, alone.

The house was dark when he brought it into sight. He halted his horse for a few moments and stared at it. He could feel his heart pounding within his chest. He could feel the racing of his blood. His hands began to shake.

Still half a mile away from the house, he turned at right angles and rode up onto the first cedar-covered ridge. He continued along it until he was well behind the house. Then he dropped out of sight behind it, dismounted and tied his horse to a clump of brush.

He walked back to the top of the ridge and laid down in a spot from which he could plainly see the dark bulk of the house below. He rolled onto his back and closed his eyes.

He slept almost instantly, but lightly, and wakened often when his ears picked up some small and alien noise. Each time he stayed awake until it was repeated, then dropped off to sleep again as soon as he was sure whatever made it did not threaten him.

In some ways, he thought drowsily after one such awakening, prison schooled a man. It taught him to sleep when the opportunity presented itself, regardless of what was going on around him. He'd been able to sleep in the dungeon whenever it became unbearable. Only by doing so had he kept himself from going mad.

He came awake as dawn began to gray the eastern sky. He heard a bucket clang in the valley below, and heard the squeak of the pump handle.

He rolled onto his stomach carefully and peered down through the gloom. There was a man at the pump, wearing pants, boots and gunbelt, but no shirt. He filled the bucket he was carrying and returned to the house with it. Shortly thereafter, a thin plume of smoke rose from the tin chimney of the place.

The light grew steadily until Varra could see each small detail of the scene below. The house was old and exactly as he remembered it. It was built of logs, freighted in, no doubt, from the high country south of town. The logs were chinked with mud and the roof was almost flat, covered with sod out of which a profusion of dry weeds grew. There was a log barn, two large pole corrals, and a collection of smaller buildings constructed as the others were.

To Varra's left, the sky turned pink and after a while the rim of the sun poked above the ragged hills. It rose steadily until its rays reached him, warming him.

The back door of the house opened and four men came out. One, the stockiest, Varra recognized as Dan.

He raised his rifle and sighted carefully. He put his sights on Dan Radek's chest, then lowered them deliberately to his belly. He held there steadily as Dan crossed the yard to the corral.

He muttered softly to himself, "Do you feel uneasy, Dan? Do you burn a little bit in your gut? You will, you dirty, son-of-a-bitch, but not today. I'm saving you for last."

Dan Radek stopped at the corral gate, hesitated, then scanned the hills around the house with a puzzled frown. Shrugging impatiently, he went into the corral and caught himself a horse. The three with him followed suit. The four saddled up, mounted and rode out of the yard, heading east toward town.

Varra didn't move. A fly began to buzz around his head, a shiny green blow-fly. Even when it lighted on his cheek, he didn't move.

Half an hour passed. At last the door opened again down below and a fifth man came out, a pan of dishwater in his hands. He threw it out on the ground, already whitened with old soap-suds immediately before the door, and went back inside.

The sun had reached the valley floor. When the man came out again, Varra recognized him as Bert, the youngest of Dan Radek's sons.

Bert had been just a boy ten years ago. He must be twenty now, Max thought. He'd do for a start even if he hadn't had a part in the business that had sent him to prison for twenty years.

The young man went to the corral and caught himself a horse. He saddled, mounted, and started down-country in the direction his father and brothers had gone.

Varra got up and ran to where his horse was tied. He mounted, whirled, and at a steady lope rode down-country to head Bert Radek off.

He stayed in the cedar hills for about three miles. Then he cut abruptly right, topped the ridge overlooking the road, and saw Bert approaching less than a mile away.

He dropped down into the valley and halted his horse in the middle of the road.

Bert saw him, but didn't hesitate. He came on steadily. When he was a dozen yards away from Max he called, "Howdy. Looking for someone?"

Max nodded, but he didn't speak.

"Who you looking for?" The young man's expression was puzzled but not yet afraid. "You."

"Me? Why me? I don't know you."

"Don't you? Take another look."

Bert rode closer, staring uncertainly at Max's face. There were the beginnings of uneasiness in him, and a touch of fear.

He looked long and hard at Varra's face, groping in his memory as he did. Varra said, "You were about ten. You were at the trial."

"Varra! Max Varra!"

"Yeah. Now you've got it."

"What . . . ?" Bert saw something in Varra's eyes that made him grab frantically for his gun.

Varra's was in his hand before Bert got his out. He placed his first shot carefully. It smashed Bert's right arm and made his gun drop from his nerveless hand.

Bert's face was suddenly gray with shock. His eyes showed pain, and shock, and unbelief. He said, "Why? I didn't. . . ."

"You're a Radek. That's enough for me."

Bert stared down at his smashed arm. Blood ran down it and dripped from his fingers onto the ground. He said, "I got to get to a doctor, fast."

"You ain't goin' to no doctor, boy." Max raised his gun again. He thumbed the hammer back deliberately.

Bert stared at him, horror dawning in his eyes. He licked his dry lips and tried to speak but nothing came out but a wordless croak. He sank spurs suddenly into the horse's sides.

The animal jumped, straight toward Max. Max fired instantly.

Bert was driven back out of the saddle. He hit the road on his back and gave a gusty grunt. But he didn't move. He lay, spread out, staring sightlessly at the sky.

Max thrust the revolver back into his belt. He cursed softly to himself. Damn it anyway. He hadn't meant it to be so quick. He'd meant to put half a dozen bullets into Bert. He'd meant to make it last. Only the damn kid had bolted and the second shot hadn't been as carefully placed as he'd planned for it to be.

He turned his head and stared down the road toward town. Dan and his other three sons probably hadn't heard the shots. But they'd be back this way sometime this afternoon. They'd pick up Max's trail.

He crossed the valley and climbed the cedar hills on the southern side. He angled toward town, but before he reached it, put his horse up the steep first ridge bordering it. He crossed this ridge, and another, and was in scattered jackpine when he struck the road.

He made no attempt to hide his trail

He wanted it to be plain and easily read. He knew they'd follow it to the Tate place and no farther. He grinned humorlessly to himself. Dan Radek would jump to the conclusion Varra wanted him to reach. He wouldn't know he'd been mistaken until Varra struck again.

Chapter Twelve

Dan Radek and his three sons worked steadily all morning. At noon they had a gather of close to eighty head.

Dan halted them, more to rest the horses than their riders. He was puzzled at Bert's failure to appear, but he was not concerned. He sat with his back to a gray shale rock and rolled a cigarette with stubby, thick fingers, the backs of which were covered with coarse hair.

Radek was as thick and stubby as his fingers. He had a broad, full face, a jutting jaw, and a forehead that was fairly shallow or perhaps only appeared so because of the broadness of his face.

His eyes were small and set close to his nose. He wore a short, trimmed beard. He said, "We'll push this bunch back to the house this afternoon. Tomorrow we'll take them up and put them on the

Tate place. We can use that grass and I'm damned if anybody's got a better right to it."

"What about Tate's girl?"

"What about her? Even if she does come back, she can't stay." He grinned. "There ain't no place for her to stay."

"You goin' to buy that land from her?"

"Maybe. If the price is right." He grinned again.

He stared at his three sons. They were all like him, he thought. In looks as well as in temperament. They were damned good kids.

He found himself wondering what had held Bert up. He remembered suddenly the strange feeling of uneasiness he had experienced at the corral this morning. He found himself wondering if there could be a connection between the two things.

He got up, snorting with self-disgust. What kind of an old woman was he turning into, anyway? What could happen to Bert?

But in spite of his own scoffings, he hurried the cattle along just a little faster than was necessary during the early part of the afternoon. Bert did not appear.

In late afternoon, driving the cattle up the lower part of the valley, Dan saw something in the road ahead.

Instantly the uneasiness he felt this morning returned. He spurred his horse and raced around the herd. He could tell before he had gone far, that what he had seen was a man, lying in the road. And he knew, even before he was close enough for recognition, that it was Bert.

He flung himself from his horse. He ran, on thick, stubby legs, to his son's side and knelt.

He did not need to feel for pulse to tell that Bert was dead. He could see the drying spot of blood on the left side of Bert's chest. He could see the bloody arm. . . .

His throat felt tight. He felt a burning sensation in his eyes. He said, "Bert!" and choked up on the word.

His eyes streaming tears, he looked up at his remaining sons. Jess asked in a tight, small voice, "He ain't dead is he, pa?"

Dan nodded wordlessly. Jess said, "But who'd do it? And why?"

Dan got up. He brushed at his eyes impatiently with the hairy back of his hand. He said, "Jess, take the cattle on up to the corral. Lew, you go to the house and get a wagon to bring Bert home. Frank, come with me. We'll get the son-of-a-bitch if it takes a week."

He walked to his horse and mounted. Lew headed for the house. Jess stared at Bert's body a moment, then rode back to start the cattle up the valley again. Dan picked up the killer's trail and followed it at a lope. Frank galloped after him.

The sun was low in the western sky. They'd probably not get very far before darkness forced them to stop, Dan thought. He glanced toward the north, at the cloudless sky. There'd be no rain to obscure the trail.

The trail angled east toward town. The killer seemed to be making no attempt to hide it, Dan noticed, and for a while this worried him because he figured the killer was heading for town, counting on his tracks being lost in the streets.

When the trail climbed the steep ridge south of town, Dan breathed a slow sigh of relief because it looked like the killer wasn't heading for town after all.

The light faded rapidly. At last, at the crest of the second ridge, Dan was forced to stop.

Fuming, he sat his horse staring in the direction the trail had been going. Frank said, "We could light a torch."

"All right. Find one. Find a dead tree and get a pitchy branch off it." He swung to the ground and dropped his horse's reins. He gathered twigs and small dead sticks until he had enough for a fire. He lighted it and watched it grow.

Frank returned with a pitch knot and Dan laid it in the fire. It took several minutes to catch, but when it did, he handed it to Frank. "Let's go. You carry that and I'll watch the trail."

More slowly now, they continued, down the slope of the ridge and on, to reach the road at last. The tracks were plainer on the bare surface of the road and Dan urged his horse into a trot.

This was the road to T Diamond, to Tate's old place, yet right now the fact meant nothing to Dan. So far as he knew, Donna Tate was gone. She had sold her cattle, taken the money and left. He didn't know where she'd gone or whether she would be back. He didn't care.

At a trot, the pair traveled steadily and the hours slowly wore away. A late rising moon came up. The pitch knot burned out.

But they could trail by moonlight now, at least in spots where the low-hanging moon put its light upon the road. And the trail did not deviate.

The two reached the lower end of T Diamond's hay meadow and here Dan stopped suddenly. There was a fire over by the gutted buildings. It was dim and hard to see because it had died to a bed of coals but it was there.

He murmured softly, "The dumb son-of-a-bitch! Didn't he think someone would follow his trail?"

Frank was silent for a long time. At last he said, "Something's wrong. Why would he lead us here? Unless . . ."

"Unless there's a bunch of 'em waiting? But who? And why?"

"Damned if I know, pa."

"Let's find out. You drop back a ways. I'll go in first."

Frank sat his horse without moving. Dan urged his on ahead. He rode to within half a mile of the fire, then dismounted and tied his horse to a tree beside the narrow road. He continued on foot, walking in the grass at the side of the road to muffle the sound of his boots.

Fifty yards from the fire he stopped. He slipped his gun from its holster and thumbed the hammer back. He stared at the shadows around the glowing fire. He saw two lumped shapes, no more.

The same uneasiness that had troubled him early this morning began to trouble him again. Something about this wasn't right. He felt the hairs on the back of his neck stir, felt the skin there tingling.

Then he thought of Bert, of the smashed arm, of the blood . . . He remembered Bert's dead face, colorless, waxen. . . .

He went on, as carefully, as silently as a stalking cat. Each time he put his foot down it was upon previously tested ground, and he made no sound.

He was still fifteen feet from the fire when one of the lumped shapes reared up. Dan snapped harshly, "Don't reach for nothin', mister. Just stand up so I can look at you."

The shape stood up. The other stirred and came up too. Dan said, "One of you put some wood on the fire."

The smaller of the two shapes approached the fire, knelt and put more wood on it. It smoked furiously several moments, then burst into flame.

By the light, Dan recognized Donna Tate. The other, the man, he didn't know. But the whole thing began to make sense now. Donna had hired herself a killer. A killer, certainly, but an incredibly stupid one.

From the darkness behind Dan, Frank's voice called, "You all right, pa?"

"I'm all right. Come on in."

Frank walked into the circle of light. The man with Donna asked, "What the hell is this all about?"

"Shut up! You know what it's all about. We followed your tracks here from the place you gunned Bert down."

The man was big and powerful. His face said that he was tough, able, smart. It didn't add up with what he'd done, but right now Radek didn't care. This man was going to die.

He asked, "What's your name?"

"Sands." The voice was calm, steady, self-assured.

The tone angered Radek enormously. Damn him, Sands didn't even have enough sense to be afraid. It suddenly became important to Radek that he make Sands admit his crime.

He stepped close to Sands. He swung his right hand and smashed the gun against the side of Sands' face. The man staggered to one side and fell.

Donna Tate gasped with protest at the brutality of it. Radek stepped to Sands and kicked him savagely in the stomach.

Sands rolled. He came to his knees, shaking his head. Blood streamed from his left ear and from a gash on his left cheekbone. He raised a hand and brushed at it. Then he wiped the bloody hand on his trouser leg. He got carefully to his feet. His eyes smoldered as he stared at Dan.

That angered Dan more than his calmness had. He swung the gun again.

Sands caught his wrist. Behind Dan, Frank yelled, "Leggo, you bastard!" and fired into the air.

Sands released Dan's wrist. Dan stepped back, raising his gun. He'd kill Sands now. But first he'd break the man. He'd put bullets into both his arms, into his legs too if it was necessary. Before Sands died, he was going to beg.

There was a flurry of movement beside the fire. He swung his gun that way. . . .

Sands moved with surprising swiftness for his size. He crashed into Dan and bowled him back. . . . Dan fell and Sands was on him like a wolf.

Dan heard a gunshot from the direction of the fire. His own gun discharged as Sands tried to tear it out of his hand. Frank yelled something frantically, something Dan didn't understand.

He fought with savage desperation but he was no match for Sands. The man wrenched the gun from his grasp and clipped him on top of the head with it. Then Sands pushed himself away and got up, holding the gun.

Radek struggled to his feet. Donna Tate stood beside the fire, a rifle in her hands. Frank had dropped his gun and now stood with his hands half raised. There was a growing spot of fresh blood on his sleeve above the elbow.

Sands said harshly, "I don't know what the hell this is all about. But you two get your horses and ride."

Dan's head felt as though it were bursting. Frank's face was gray with the shock of his wound. Dan said,

"Come on, Frank." He turned and tramped away into the darkness. Frank followed him, shuffling along as though he were in a daze.

Behind him, at the fire, there was no sound.

Sands didn't move until the sounds of the two horses had died completely away. Then he turned his head and looked at Donna.

She was shaking violently. Her lower lip trembled and her eyes glistened with unshed tears. He said, "You . . . thanks."

She did not reply. Stiffly, as though holding her control with difficulty, she laid the rifle down against one of the saddles. Sands said, "Looks like Varra's gone to work."

"And he led them here."

He nodded.

"The sheriff will be coming with a posse next."

"Maybe not. Maybe Radek will try to handle it himself."

"He has two other sons. You can't fight four of them."

"Maybe I won't have to. I'll be leaving in a day or two."

"Leave now. Tonight. I don't want you to get mixed up with this."

He stared at her. She said spiritedly, "You don't owe me anything. I didn't get you out of Yuma. You got yourself out. Take your horse and go."

"You *want* me to leave?"

She hesitated a moment, then nodded determinedly.

Yet in her eyes, as she looked up at him, there was panic at the thought.

He discovered that he didn't want to leave. He said, "I'll stick around until I get that cabin built. Then we'll see."

"Please. It will be too late by then."

He shrugged. "Maybe. Maybe not. Anyhow, I'm not going to leave."

He went to the fire and squatted beside it. He stared into the flames as his hand went automatically to his pocket and withdrew the tobacco sack and packet of papers. He rolled himself a smoke.

He knew he was a fool for staying here. He forced himself to think of Yuma, of the pit, of the stench, the brutality, the ceaseless, unbearable heat. He made himself remember how it felt to be chained like an animal to a line of other men, many of whom *were* animals.

He'd go back to that if he stayed. Or he'd die. He glanced up at Donna Tate, who was watching him.

Something passed between them, something that stirred conflicting feelings in him. He knew he wanted her; he also knew he could not trust that feeling in itself. She was a woman. It probably was no more than that. And he was a man who had been long deprived.

There were other places, better places than this, to which he could go. He could change his appearance. He could lose himself. He need never return to Yuma if he planned carefully enough.

Yet he remained unconvinced. He wanted to stay here.

He finished his cigarette and flung it into the fire. He watched it quickly consumed, struck by a parallel as it was. His own freedom would be as short lived if he stayed.

His jaw firmed stubbornly. He laid down and stared up at the sky.

Donna Tate watched him for a long, long time, her face softening gradually as she did. Then, without speaking, she laid down where she had been before and pillowed her head on her saddle. She watched Owen steadily until she fell asleep.

Chapter Thirteen

It was well after midnight when Dan Radek, followed by his son Frank, rode up the valley and stopped before the sod-roofed house. Jess and Lew both came to the door carrying rifles. A lamp burned in the living room that served as a kitchen too.

Dan said harshly, "Jess, put the horses up," and stamped inside. He threw his hat on the table, hesitated a moment, then went into the room where Bert's body lay. He closed the door behind him.

It was dark in here. He fumbled for a match, struck it and lighted the lamp on the dresser. He trimmed the wick, then turned to stare at Bert. He felt a burning behind his eyes, a tightness in his throat.

Affection was something a man didn't show toward

his grown sons, but that didn't mean it wasn't there. He crossed the room to the bedside.

Suddenly he sank to his knees beside the bed. He buried his face in his dead son's chest. His body shook soundlessly.

He remained this way for a long, long time. Then he rose. He crossed the room to the door and opened it. His three remaining sons met his glance soberly.

Dan said, "Lew, come sit with your brother."

"Sure, pa." Lew hurriedly crossed the room, sidled around Dan and went into the bedroom.

Dan said, "Jess, fix us something to eat."

Jess immediately went to the stove and began to build up the fire. Dan crossed to Frank and without speaking, helped him remove his shirt. He lifted the teakettle, which was simmering on the back of the stove, and poured some water into a pan. He began to wash Frank's gunshot wound.

It was a flesh wound, in the upper part of the arm, no more than a deep gouge actually. But Frank's face turned pale as he worked.

When he had washed the wound, Dan got a bottle of whisky from a cupboard. He uncorked it and handed it to Frank. "Take a big drink."

Frank tilted the bottle and took several gulping swallows. He began to cough as he lowered it. Dan took it from him and poured whisky over the bleeding, ragged wound. Frank's face turned gray, but he did not pass out.

Dan steadied him for several moments. Then he disappeared into another room and returned, carrying a clean flour sack, which he ripped into strips. He began to bandage the wound, winding the strips around and around the arm. Finished, he ripped the last strip lengthwise, tied it, then wound it around the arm and tied it again. He said, "Go to bed. It'll hurt like bloody hell for a while."

Frank nodded. He picked up the bottle and took another drink. He got up and staggered into the bedroom he had shared with Lee before Lee was killed several months before.

Dan lighted a lantern. Carrying it, he went outside.

There was a pile of used lumber at one side of the log barn. He gathered up a number of boards and went into the barn. He hung the lantern up, then got a saw, a hammer and a keg of nails.

He worked steadily for more than an hour, measuring, sawing, hammering. When he was finished he had a rough pine coffin with a hinged lid.

He dragged it outside and across the yard to the door. He raised one end and leaned it against the house. Then he went inside.

He sat down at the table and stared blankly into space. Jess filled a plate for him and brought it to him, along with a steaming mug of coffee. Dan ate, though the food seemed to make an undigestible ball in his stomach. Afterward, he went back into the bedroom where his dead son lay. He nodded at Lew. "Go get something to eat. I'll sit with him."

Lew glanced at his face and glanced away. He went

quietly from the room, closing the door behind him.

Dan sat silently, staring at his dead son's face until dawn began to gray the sky.

Dan Radek rode in the lead. Lew followed, driving the buckboard in which the plain, pine casket lay. Jess and Frank rode behind the buckboard, abreast.

All four were dressed in their best. Dan's suit was black. Those of his sons were varying shades of brown.

Instead of their usual, battered wide-brimmed hats, all four wore black derby hats. All wore stiff celluloid collars and ties. They entered town at eight o'clock, a slow processional that filed steadily toward the small white church at the foot of the hill on the southern rim of town.

Half a dozen small boys ran alongside the procession. The townspeople turned to stare as it went past. The sheriff came out of his office and watched but did not call out. His face was grim. After the buckboard had passed, he went into his office, got his hat, then followed the Radeks toward the church.

The minister came out of his neat frame house which nestled in the shadow of the church. He went back inside hastily and came out again, wearing his black coat and carrying a Bible in his hand. He opened the doors of the church and waited in front of them.

The buckboard drew to a halt in front. Dan dismounted solemnly and tied his horse. Jess and Frank followed suit. All four of the Radeks gathered at the rear of the buckboard and slid the coffin out. Carrying it, they came up the dusty walk to the tiny church.

Without speaking, they carried the coffin inside, up the aisle, and placed it on the raised platform at the front of the church. The four then sat down in the front pew and waited patiently.

The minister, a tall, dour man named Crispe, glanced helplessly at the sheriff as he entered the church. Will Purdy nodded at him. Crispe walked slowly to the front of the church, climbed the steps and began to read. "I am the resurrection and the light. Whosoever believeth in me shall live, even though he be dead. . . ."

He read tonelessly for about ten minutes. When he stopped, Dan Radek and his sons stood up. They silently lifted the casket and carried it out. They loaded it in the buckboard.

Purdy stopped Dan before he could mount his horse. He asked, "What happened, Dan?"

"Bert's dead."

"How'd he die?"

"Shot."

Purdy gave a patient sigh. "I don't want to interfere with your funeral, Dan. But if you don't tell me about it, I'll have to interfere."

"We'll take care of it ourselves."

"That's exactly what I don't want you to do. Frank's been shot too, hasn't he?"

Dan nodded.

"Who shot him?"

Dan turned blazing eyes on him. "That little Tate bitch shot him. Last night."

"You don't mean to tell me she killed Bert?"

"Huh uh. She's brought a killer back with her."

"All right Dan. Go on."

Dan mounted. Lew climbed to the buckboard seat. The other two swung to their horses and fell in behind.

The procession left town as it had entered, slowly, solemnly. Scowling, Purdy walked back toward his office. He had a little time. It would take Dan and his sons the best part of the day to return home, dig a grave and bury Bert. But when that was done, the four would be riding south toward Tate's. It was up to him to get there first.

The street was fairly crowded now, crowded for a town the size of Cutbank at least. Will stopped to speak to someone several times on his way to the jail. Each time he paused only long enough to say, "I want you for a posse. Get a horse and meet in front of the jail at ten."

He reached the jail and stopped on the walk in front to light a cigar. He puffed thoughtfully for several moments, struck by the Radeks' inconsistency. They'd wanted a church funeral service for Bert. Yet to Purdy's knowledge they had never attended church in their lives. Only once before, when Lee was killed, had they ever been inside.

With Bert safely in the ground . . . they would become as savage as animals in their quest for revenge. Just as they had when Lee was killed, when they'd hanged Jake Tate.

He stared at the street sourly. They'd been acquitted of hanging Jake. There'd been no evidence. But Purdy had known they were guilty of it. So had almost everyone else in town.

He thought briefly of Donna Tate. It didn't surprise him to learn that she'd brought a killer back. Actually he couldn't blame her much. The law had certainly failed her.

Now the law was going to have to take the Radeks' side. The thought left a sour taste in Purdy's mouth.

He threw the cigar away. He stamped angrily toward the livery barn.

He got his horse, saddled and bridled him and led him up the street. Several of his possemen were waiting in front of the jail. Purdy spoke to one of them, "Willie, go over to Delaney's and get a sack full of grub. Enough to last six men three days."

Willie Pierce mounted and rode away up-street. Purdy nervously lighted another cigar.

One after another of his possemen arrived. When Willie Pierce returned, all five were here.

Mostly they were silent, but every now and then one of them would say something to the others in a lowered, indistinguishable tone. Purdy went inside and got five rifles out of the rack beside the door. He carried them out and handed them, one by one, to his possemen. He returned for a couple of boxes of cartridges. He gave each man a handful and dumped the remainder in one of his saddle bags.

He said, "Donna Tate is back. She brought a killer with her. He shot Bert yesterday and Dan and Frank trailed him to Tate's. Donna shot at Frank and nicked him in the arm."

One of the men said, "Serves the bastards right."

Purdy put a steady glance on the man. "Maybe. Maybe that trial a while back didn't come out right. But this ain't the way to do things. We're going to bring that killer in and hold him for trial."

No one spoke. Purdy mounted and led them south out of town. He rode at a steady trot until he reached the steepest part of the grade. Here he let his horse slow to a walk. Twice before he reached the top of the ridge, he stopped to let the horses blow.

He remembered the stranger he'd talked to yesterday in town. He wondered if the man was Donna Tate's killer and felt a sudden, wry disillusionment with himself. He'd liked the stranger in spite of the hard look of the man. If the stranger turned out to be Bert Radek's killer he ought to turn in his badge. If he couldn't judge men any better than that he was getting too old for the sheriff's job.

And there was another thing. Delaney's store had been broken into night before last. A couple of guns had disappeared. He frowned confusedly. He'd seen the stranger buying stuff in Delaney's the morning after the robbery. If he'd robbed the place he wouldn't have needed to come back. Nor would he have showed himself and his stolen guns in town.

His mind seized on that hopefully. Maybe there was more than one stranger hereabouts. Maybe the man wasn't guilty after all.

He abandoned his sudden hope dismally. It didn't matter whether the man was guilty or not. He'd have to find him, arrest him and hold him in jail. Otherwise the Radeks would kill him. Or he'd kill one or more of them fighting back.

He reached the forks and rode a dozen yards beyond. Then he stopped and got down off his horse. He studied the tracks in the road.

The tracks of the horses ridden by Dan and Frank were here, coming toward town. Older, but still plain, were the tracks the stranger had made coming to town with his pack animal, returning without him.

He mounted again, frowning. He rode on, studying the road, until he came to the place where three more sets of tracks entered the road.

He dismounted again, and studied them. Two sets of the tracks he recognized as belonging to the horses of Dan and Frank. The other. . . .

He walked slowly back to where this trail entered the road. He backtracked across the mountain side, occasionally stopping to kneel close and study one of the prints. When he returned to his men he said, "That's a different horse than he rode to town yesterday. Or else it's a different man."

Mounted again, he continued, but the frown of puzzlement did not leave his face. For he had noticed something else. There had been no attempt on the part of the killer to conceal his trail.

At the lower end of the Tate meadow, Purdy stopped and raised a hand to halt his men. He said, "There'll be no gunplay, understand? I want him, but I ain't quite satisfied. I sure as hell don't want him dead."

He thought most of the men seemed relieved, and he supposed it was natural enough that they were. There wasn't a one of them who didn't think the Radeks guilty of hanging Jake Tate, regardless of what the court had said. One of them, Les Sparks, had even been a juryman.

He said, "All right then, let's get this over with." He touched his horse's sides with his heels and trotted him toward the gutted buildings half a mile away.

He could see Donna, standing in the sun, shading her eyes against the glare. He saw her turn her head and moments later heard her shrill cry of warning to the man.

He kicked his horse into a run. Behind him, the five possemen followed suit.

He still didn't see the man. He saw the logs that had been accumulated at the bottom of the hill. He saw the beginnings of a small cabin nearby.

And he caught a glimpse of the brown rump of a horse just as it disappeared into thick timber a quarter mile above where Donna stood.

126

He hauled his plunging horse to a halt in front of her. He waved his men on and they plunged up the hillside in pursuit.

At this moment he was thinking, "Maybe Dan was right. If he hadn't killed Bert, why the hell would he think he had to run?"

Chapter Fourteen

White-faced and furious, Donna Tate stared up at the sheriff. "You're always right on the job when someone does something to the Radeks, aren't you, Mr. Purdy? But where were you when this was done?" She gestured angrily toward the burned buildings.

Purdy said, "I'm sorry, Donna."

"Sorry? Sorry doesn't help. It didn't help when my father was killed. It doesn't help now."

"Who is he? The man you brought back?"

"You seem to know that already. You know enough about him to want him for killing Bert."

"Who told you Bert was dead?"

"Dan Radek was here last night with Frank."

"Who shot Frank? You or him?"

"I did. And next time I'll shoot straighter than I did last night."

He stared down at her helplessly. Conflicting feelings battled within his mind—anger because the law was being flaunted—shame because of the injustice done when the Radeks were acquitted of killing Jake Tate and because these buildings had been burned and he'd not been able to tie it to anyone.

He didn't blame Donna for her attitude. But neither could he allow the law to be bypassed. The law wasn't perfect. But it was better than nothing. And in the end. . . .

He said, "What's the man's name?"

"Sands. Owen Sands."

"Where'd you find him?"

He thought her expression became evasive. She said, "What does that matter? I needed someone. I can't fight the Radeks by myself."

"Then you brought him here to fight the Radeks for you?"

"I didn't say that. But I can tell you one thing. He didn't kill Bert. He was here, cutting logs. He's only been away from here once and that was when he went to Cutbank for supplies."

"The trail led here."

She looked at him pityingly. "Do you think he'd be fool enough to kill Bert and then make a trail back here?"

This had been bothering Purdy all along. It didn't make sense. He had met Sands in town and knew the man was not a fool. He asked suddenly, "Is Sands the only one you brought back with you?"

She looked suddenly at the ground. She nodded wordlessly.

Purdy knew she was lying. He glanced up the hillside. His men were out of sight but he could still hear them crashing through the trees. He touched his horse's sides with his heels and trotted him up the long meadow. He did not look back.

He was frowning as he rode. Donna had lied to him a few moments before. Sands was not the only one she had brought back with her.

The other man, then, must be the one who had murdered Bert. But why would he lead the Radeks straight to Donna and to Sands? Unless he hated them?

More confused, even, than before, he came abreast of the crashing noises above him in the timber and turned his horse that way. He climbed steadily until he struck the broad trail they had made. He turned into it, drumming on his horse's sides with his heels, wishing he had spurs. Half an hour later, he caught up with the other five.

They were halted on a ridge top, staring down into a heavily timbered valley ahead of them. One said, "We caught a glimpse of him just a few minutes ago. He's ridin' a barebacked horse with harness on."

Purdy stared ahead at the rough, timbered country. It raised steadily from here to a range of bare peaks in the dim distance, peaks that were still spotted with last winter's snow. He'd find out soon if the man he was pursuing was a fool—fool enough to make trail from the Radeks' place to Tate's.

He rode down the south side of the ridge, following Sands' trail. Sometimes he was forced to slow when the trail crossed a stretch of bare broken rock. He realized that Sands had not yet begun what attempts he might make later to hide it from pursuit.

The day wore steadily away. They caught no further glimpse of Sands. Purdy guessed the man was at least a mile ahead.

Well after noon, they reached a rushing mountain stream, one called No Name Creek. Here, Sands' trail went into the water, angling upstream as it did.

Purdy halted his men. He rode his horse into the stream. He rode upstream for a quarter mile but he did not find tracks coming out on the other side. He returned and rode a similar distance downstream, with the same results.

He returned wryly to his men, "We split up here. Three of you go downstream until you find something. I'll take the other two and go upstream. If you pick up his trail, fire a couple of shots."

He went through the motions all that afternoon. He found where Sands left the stream and fired a couple of shots to advise the other three. But he knew he had lost, at least for now. He had lost if he considered that his objective had been to capture Sands.

He was not completely sure it had. He was not convinced Sands had killed Bert at all. And if his purpose had been to remove Sands from the danger of vengeance by the Radek clan, then he had succeeded in doing that.

He returned toward the Tate place, but halted at dark to rest the exhausted horses and discouraged men. He ought to camp here for the night, he thought, and knew no one would object.

Yet a strange uneasiness troubled him. He felt almost as though he had been drawn away deliberately—by someone who didn't want him around to interfere.

The Radeks' funeral procession left Cutbank and traveled deliberately west, into the maze of cedar-covered hills. Up the long valley below the house it went, not pausing until it reached the top of a small knoll behind the house.

There were three graves here, marked by low mounds of earth and by wooden crosses upon which traces of whitewash still were visible. One was the grave of Lee. Another was the grave of Radek's wife, who had died after bearing Bert. The third, its earthen mound barely discernable, was the grave of a girl baby who had died before she could be named.

The three men dismounted silently. Lew climbed down from the buckboard seat. Dan said shortly, "Frank, you get up on that buckboard. You can't dig with that arm of yours."

Frank obediently climbed to the buckboard seat. Lew and Jess got shovels out of the back. With the toe of his boot, Dan marked out a grave beside that of Lee. The two began to dig.

Dan stared gloomily down toward the house. Once he lifted his face to the horizon in the direction of town. He began to pace nervously back and forth.

He was remembering . . . and at times pain was sharp and strong in his brooding eyes. He was remembering a stranded girl, whom both he and Jake

Tate had courted. He was remembering his bitter sense of loss when she had married Jake.

He felt no shame for having resumed seeing her. He was convinced she had made a mistake in marrying Jake. What he did regret was that he hadn't killed Jake quickly the day Jake caught him with her when he came home. If he had, she might not now be dead. His whole life could have been different.

But he hadn't killed Jake. They'd fought like animals until both were exhausted and unconscious on the ground. She had died in a blizzard on the way to town.

He noted with surprise that the grave was almost three feet deep. He walked to it and said, "You two knock off for a while. I'll finish it."

He took a shovel and climbed down into the grave. He worked like a maniac, throwing out as much earth as had both his sons. He began to sweat heavily and his breath exhaled from his lungs like air coming from the bellows of a blacksmith's forge.

But exertion stopped his thoughts; it stopped the torture of his memories.

When the grave was six feet deep, he stopped. He yelled at his sons and they extended their hands so that he could get out.

He took down the lariat from his saddle horn. Jess took his down too. The four gathered at the rear of the buckboard and lifted the casket out. They laid it on the ropes, then carried it to the grave by holding to the ropes. They lowered it in carefully.

All four removed their hats. Dan said, "We'll get the son-of-a-bitch for you, Bert. Then I reckon you can rest."

Jess and Lew picked up the shovels. They began to fill in the grave. When they had finished they tossed the shovels in the back of the buckboard, then mounted and followed it down the hill.

At the house, Jess unhitched the team. Lew caught himself a saddle horse. Jess went into the house and returned, carrying a sack of food and four blanket rolls.

The four mounted and rode down the valley in the direction of town. This time, they stayed on the road, passed through town riding four abreast along its busy street, then on beyond up the road that led to the Tate ranch.

Riding through town had been deliberate. Dan Radek was serving notice on the townspeople and on the sheriff's office that henceforth he was taking this into his own hands, giving them a thinly veiled warning not to interfere.

In the late afternoon he reached the forks, riding at a steady trot. At sundown he rode into the valley below the burned ranch buildings belonging to Donna Tate.

Here, he dispersed his sons. Two of them he sent on ahead, riding on the timbered hillside out of sight. He waited, gave them fifteen minutes to allow them to get well ahead of him. Then he and Frank rode on up the road.

Donna met them, a rifle in her hands, a worried look in her eyes. She said, "That's far enough."

"Where is he?"

"He's gone. The sheriff's chasing him."

"Alone?"

"He has a posse. Five men from town."

Dan felt a sudden, balked fury. Damn Purdy anyhow! Why the hell didn't he stay out of it?

He stared down at Donna. He hadn't hated her mother but he hated her. She was a living reminder of the nights Jake Tate had spent with Martha here. She was a living reminder of that union. . . .

He felt wildness possessing him and did nothing to beat it down. It rose with reckless abandon until at last he knew he was going to kill this girl. With her dead, there would be nothing left to remind him of the past. Once she was dead, the dead and the half dead memories could rest.

He heard a twig crack over beyond the burned buildings. He glanced that way and saw Lew and Jess riding out of the timber. Donna watched his face, wanting to turn her head but fearing to.

Dan said, "You can put down that gun. Lew and Jess just rode out of the timber behind you."

"You're lying."

Dan looked at his two sons. He said, "Sing out, Lew. You too, Jess."

"Sure, pa." They said it in unison.

Dan stared steadily at Donna. Her face was white and there was something close to panic in her eyes.

Her shoulders sagged. She put the rifle down, leaning it against the pile of logs.

Dan swung off his horse. He walked over, picked the rifle up and threw it violently toward the gutted buildings. His face was white but his eyes were blazing when he turned. "Who is he? Where'd you hire him?"

She didn't speak. Dan's hand lashed out like a striking rattler. It struck the side of her face and she fell in a crumpled heap. Dan said, "You little bitch, that's only a sample of what I'm going to do to you. Now talk. Who is he and where'd you find him? Why'd you bring him here, to gun us down one by one?"

She looked up at him. There was terror in her eyes but they were as implacable as the icy cold that had taken her mother's life. He stooped and yanked her to her feet. Holding her with one hand, he slapped her face repeatedly with the other. Her eyes closed and her body slumped.

The light was fading in the sky. The afterglow of the setting sun lay on a few high clouds. Soon it would be dark.

He let Donna fall. He said harshly, "Lew, get me some water from the creek."

Lew poked around among the gear in camp until he found a blackened pan. He walked to the creek, filled it and brought it back. Dan took it from him and dumped it squarely in Donna's face. Gasping and choking, she sat up.

Dan was suddenly tired of this, tired of asking questions she wouldn't answer anyway. He asked, "You know what I'm going to do, don't you?"

She nodded. Frank's voice came in a shocked protest. "Pa, you can't. . . ."

Dan raised his gun. He pointed it at Donna's head and thumbed the hammer back.

He never fired. Jess pitched forward, as though he had been kicked by a horse. Dan yanked his head around. . . .

The report reached him then, sonorously shouting down the timbered hill and echoing back from the taller one on the valley's other side.

Dan bawled, "After him! Hurry! It's already getting dark!"

Frank and Lew leaped to their horse's backs and thundered away up the hill. Dan knelt at Jess's side.

Blood had already drenched the front of Jess's shirt. His face was as colorless as wax. Jess was dead.

Dan gave Donna one last baleful glance. Then he swung to the back of his horse and thundered after his two remaining sons.

Chapter Fifteen

Ahead of him, Dan Radek could hear an almost frantic crashing in the thick timber. He raked his horse mercilessly, continuously with his spurs. The terrified animal lunged up the hillside, giving every bit of his strength to it.

The sky was now almost wholly gray. The after-glow on the high clouds had faded, through all the color ranges between pink and gray.

In Dan, fury was a towering, monstrous, overpowering thing, the more awful because he knew he would not catch his man tonight. It was too late. The man had planned it that way. Unless some miraculous, unbelievable chance favored the three Radeks, the killer would get away.

Sands must have circled back, he thought. Pursued by the sheriff's posse, he must have circled back, timing it so that he would arrive at dusk.

However he tried, however he raked his horse's sides, he could not catch up with his two sons. But he could hear them. And sometimes he could hear the killer, crashing through the timber ahead of them.

Objects began to blur in the fading light. Dan's mouth worked continuously and from his lips poured a steady stream of profanities. Once, he pounded helplessly on the pommel of his saddle with a tight-clenched fist.

His horse stumbled and nearly fell. Dan yanked his head up and spurred him again savagely.

But it was no use. In another five minutes it would be too dark to see. He opened his mouth and bawled, "Frank! Lew! Can't you see him? Shoot the son-of-a-bitch! Shoot him!"

He heard an answering shout, but he could not make out the words. And then he heard a shot.

For an instant, his heart seemed to stop. A terrible, wonderful exultation flooded him. They'd got him! They'd got the dirty. . . .

The crashing sounds immediately ahead of him stopped abruptly. He could still hear the fugitive, but those sounds were fading rapidly. And there was no sound from either of his sons. . . .

Terror touched his heart. The awful possibility that the killer had somehow gotten both Lew and Frank occurred to him. Then reason reasserted itself. There had been only one shot. He'd heard only one. No matter how lucky the man might have been, he couldn't have gotten them both.

He reached the two. Lew was on the ground, cursing steadily, bent over, cutting the leg of his pants with a knife. Frank still sat his horse, and was staring with startled surprise at Lew.

Lew looked up at Dan. "He got me," he said numbly. "The bastard got me in the leg."

Dan slid off his horse. There was a sudden slump in his shoulders. He wanted to lash out savagely at his sons because they had let the man get away, yet he knew they had done all they could. Even if they hadn't stopped, they couldn't possibly have overtaken Sands.

He said with dangerous calmness. "How bad is it?"

"It hurts like hell. And it's bleeding pretty bad."

Dan knelt and looked at the wound. It was ragged where the bullet had emerged, neat and even where it had entered the flesh. But it hadn't struck the bone.

That was the important thing. It hadn't struck the bone.

He yanked a bandanna from his pocket. He tied it tightly around the wound. He said, "I'll help you on your horse. There ain't much I can do in the dark. We'll get you home. . . ."

He helped Lew to get back on his horse. He mounted his own. Whoever the killer was, he had exacted a terrible toll from the Radek family in the past two days. He had killed Bert and Jess. He had wounded Frank and Lew. And he was still free. To strike from ambush any time he wished.

He led out down the hill. He wouldn't stop long down there where he'd left Donna Tate, but if he saw her as he passed. . . .

Nothing was going to restrain him from here on out. No one was going to stand in his way. Donna Tate was going to die, for bringing that killer back. The killer was going to die. If Will Purdy got in the way, then he'd die too.

He reached the bottom of the hill. Donna Tate was not beside the fire. She was nowhere to be seen.

Dan dismounted beside Jess's body. Frank rode to Jess's horse and caught up the reins.

Dan lifted his son's body almost as easily as he had when Jess had been a child. He laid him gently across his saddle, face down. He took down Jess's lariat and tied it around his booted ankles. He clove-hitched it around the saddle horn, then half-hitched it around Jess's chest. He brought the rope around under the horse's belly and tied it to his son's feet again.

He took the reins of Jess's horse from Frank. Then he led out, down the valley toward Cutbank.

It was now completely dark. Stars twinkled in a nearly cloudless sky.

Dan's head sank forward until his chin rested on his chest. He appeared to be dozing but he was not. His body, every nerve, every muscle of it was tense. His fury was like a banked fire now, diminished but still alive.

Behind him rode Lew, and Frank brought up the rear. Every now and then, Lew would grunt softly with pain as the horse's gait wrenched his wounded leg.

Dan still found it hard to believe—that Donna Tate's vengeance could have been so devastating. That it had succeeded so easily. That that killer had done this appalling amount of damage without once being shot in return.

The miles fell steadily behind. Jess's body lolled limply back and forth on his horse's back. Lew began to shiver with the cold, and the sound of his teeth chattering was an accompaniment to the sound of the wind stirring in the pines, to the sound of the rushing stream.

They reached the forks and started down. The lights of the town twinkled in the distance.

Dan suddenly remembered another night, not so very long ago, when he and his four sons had seen the twinkling lights from here. That had been the night he'd burned the buildings of the Tate place. He'd thought when he did that she would not come back. He'd thought that eventually he could forget.

But she had come back, and she'd brought with her a terrible retribution for her father's death.

Lew whimpered occasionally as they started down the steep grade toward town. They reached the bottom. Dan led his sons down the center of the town's main street. Let the damn town know that he'd been hurt. Let them know he meant to fight back. Let them understand that they were to keep their noses out of it.

Men came from the saloons to stare at the grim cavalcade. They stood silently on the walk while the Radeks passed, but as soon as they had, they buzzed with talk.

Dan and his sons left the lights of the town behind. They took the long, dark road toward home. There'd be no funeral in town for Jess, Dan thought. They'd build a casket tonight and bury him while it still was dark. When dawn came, they'd be on guard, ready, and when the killer showed up again . . . By God, next time he showed up he was going to wish he'd never heard the Radek name.

It was past midnight when the three reached home. Dan tied the horse on which Jess's body lay. He said harshly, "Come on inside, Lew. First thing I'm going to do is fix your leg. Then I want you to get some sleep. I want you up and ready to go at dawn."

"Sure, pa." Lew went in and Dan followed him. Frank started to come in after them, but Dan turned his head and said, "Take a shovel and go up on the hill. Dig Jess a grave."

Frank disappeared toward the barn. Lew went in and Dan followed. Dan found the lamp and lighted it. Lew took off his pants.

He sat down in a straight-backed chair. Dan lifted his leg and propped it up on another chair.

He cut the underwear away with his knife. He got the whisky bottle and gave Lew a drink. Then he washed the wound and poured whisky over it.

Lew passed out and fell off the chair onto the floor. Cursing softly, Dan picked him up and carried him in to his bed. He finished bandaging the wound on the blood-drenched bed, then pulled the covers over his son and returned to the kitchen. He lighted the lantern and went out to the barn.

He was tired and near exhaustion, but his anger kept him going. He measured and sawed and hammered, until at last he had the casket done. He went out, caught and harnessed the buckboard team, then loaded the casket and drove to where Jess's horse was tied.

He untied the rope and eased the body down. It was stiff and hard to manage, but he eventually got it into the casket and got the lid in place.

Suddenly he ran out into the darkness, into the middle of the yard. He bent double, cramping, retching. When he straightened, he was bathed with sweat.

Cursing softly, sick and exhausted, he returned to the house to wait for Frank.

Will Purdy reached town about an hour before dawn. The town was sleeping and he could see no lights anywhere.

He halted in front of the jail and turned his head wearily to speak to his men. "Go on home and get some sleep."

They dispersed, disappearing into the darkness almost immediately. He heard the sounds of their horses' hoofs for a while, and then even that was gone.

He dismounted stiffly and tied his horse. He went inside and built a fire in the small office stove to take the chill out of the air. He lighted the lamp and sank down dispiritedly into his swivel chair. He stared at his cluttered desk unseeingly.

The office began to warm up and a line of gray appeared along the eastern horizon. Purdy got up and went to the door. He could see a light now, up at the hotel.

He went out and tramped toward it, his feet echoing hollowly on the board walk. He went into the lobby, through the dining-room and into the kitchen where Clem Dennis, wearing a soiled apron, was beginning to start breakfast preparations. The smell of coffee was strong in the air and Purdy sank down into a chair and asked, "Coffee done, Clem?"

"Think so. If you don't want it strong as lye."

Purdy accepted a mug from him and sipped it. He was tired all the way to his bones, but he knew he'd get no sleep today.

Dennis drew a cup for himself and stood sipping it, watching the sheriff worriedly. "You catch him, Will?"

Purdy shook his head.

"Well, he caught another of the Radek bunch. Jess this time. Dan an' Frank an' Lew came riding through town around midnight, trailin' his body behind."

Purdy's shoulders sagged slightly, but he did not reply. His earlier guess . . . that Donna had brought two men back with her . . . was now confirmed. Sands could not possibly have returned to the Tate place in time to shoot another of the Radeks at the time of night it had been done. There had to be another man.

But who? And why?

The why wasn't difficult to guess. Donna wanted revenge for the hanging of her father. She wanted revenge against the whole Radek clan and if he didn't catch the killer soon, she'd get it, too. The man was going to wipe out the whole damned bunch of them, the way things were going now.

He finished his coffee, but he did not get up. He could imagine the state Dan Radek was in. He'd be like a wounded wolf, fangs bared, ready to lash out at anything that came in range. They'd bury Jess tonight, and first thing in the morning would head for Donna's place. No telling what they'd do to her. . . .

He got up reluctantly. There was only one way to

144

keep Donna safe, and that was to take her into protective custody.

Clem said, "You'd better get some sleep. You look beat."

Purdy grinned sparingly. "I am. But I'll get no sleep today." He went out into the chill dawn and walked heavily back to the jail. He went in, blew out the lamp and closed the damper on the stove. He came out again and led his horse toward the livery barn.

The place was deserted. He fed and watered the horse, then caught a fresh one out of the corral and changed the saddle and bridle to him. He led him out front and climbed to the saddle heavily. He ought to hire a deputy, he thought, a younger man, someone who could lose a little sleep without feeling so beat because of it.

He headed gloomily toward the Tate place, wondering how all this was going to end.

Not only did he have a wounded and thoroughly angered Radek clan to cope with. He also had a killer loose. And there was Sands, though where he fitted into this, Purdy didn't know.

He dozed in the saddle as he rode. Each time he jerked awake it was only to realize the mountainous complexity of the situation facing him. And to feel a hopeless uncertainty wholly strange to him.

Chapter Sixteen

The sun was an hour high in the morning sky when Dan Radek and his two remaining sons rode into Cutbank. Dan rode in the lead. Frank followed and Lew brought up the rear. Dan rode straight to the sheriff's office and swung down from his horse.

His clothes were filthy and his eyes were red. There was an unaccustomed slackness about his mouth, but his fury was unmistakable.

He went in without knocking, glanced around, then crossed the room and touched the stove. It was still warm.

Dan walked through the door at the rear and into the cellblock, his hand lightly touching the grips of his holstered gun. The cells were empty too.

Purdy hadn't caught the killer, then. He'd probably lost the trail. And as soon as he had, the killer had returned to Donna Tate's place, where he had murdered Jess.

Dan returned to the office. He went outside and mounted his horse. He'd meant to serve Purdy an ultimatum, but it would have to wait. Purdy must be at home, asleep.

He led south out of town, taking the road to Donna's place. As he rode, his smoldering anger grew. Donna was behind it all, he thought. She was the one who had brought that killer here. She had directed the murders of his sons. Today, she was going to pay for it.

Then he was going to take that killer's trail. And stay with it until the man was dead.

Purdy reached Donna's place about seven o'clock. There was a fire going. She made a small, helpless looking figure crouching over it. She glanced up at him, left the fire to pick up her rifle, then waited, the rifle cradled in her arms.

She was apparently alone. Nearby a small log cabin had been started, though the walls were only four feet high. There was a good-sized pile of logs not far away.

He rode to her and dismounted stiffly. He said, "Mornin', Donna."

She nodded at him. Her eyes were hostile.

"Got any coffee?"

"Help yourself."

He poured himself a cup of coffee and sipped it, hunkered on his heels. Donna did not relax. Neither did she lower her gun.

He said, "The Radeks will be back today. You know that, don't you?"

She did not reply.

He said, "Bert's been killed and so has Jess. Old Dan's liable to do anything now."

"Like hang me, sheriff? The way he did my father?"

"Maybe. I want you to let me take you into custody. That's the only way you're going to be safe."

"If they show up here, I'm going to shoot first and ask questions afterward."

"There are three of them. You can't. . . ."

"Maybe I'll have help."

"Who'd you bring back with you, Donna? There was more than one, wasn't there?"

"What makes you say that?"

"I trailed Sands all day yesterday. He was too far away to have gotten back here in time to shoot Jess. There had to be someone else. Someone who broke into Delaney's store to get a couple of guns and some supplies. Where'd you go when you left here, Donna? Who'd you bring back with you?"

Her mouth firmed out stubbornly. She did not reply.

He studied her, seeing now for the first time the bluish bruise on one side of her face. He asked, "Where'd you get that bruise?"

Her eyes blazed suddenly. "From Dan Radek. Last night. He was about to shoot me when Jess was killed."

"Then that settles it. You're going to come with me."

She stared at him, her eyes filled with contempt that cut him like a whip. "That's the easy way, isn't it, Mr. Purdy? You can arrrest women. You're tough enough for that. But not tough enough to arrest killers and arsonists."

He flushed painfully, aware that her accusation was not without some truth.

"Why don't you arrest Dan Radek and his sons?"

"For what? Nobody saw them burn you out. I'd never make it stick in court."

"Is it legal for men to beat women and threaten them?"

"You know it's not."

"Then arrest Radek for doing that. He hanged my father and burned me out, and got away with it. But maybe you can put him in jail for a little thing like this." She fingered the bruise resentfully.

"It wouldn't have been a little thing if your killer hadn't cut loose right then. And even if I arrest Dan, his two sons will still be loose. I wish you'd come with me, Donna. It's the only way I can be sure you're safe."

"I won't go. So you'd just as well go back to town."

Purdy stared at her helplessly, gauging the determination in her eyes. He could take her by force, he supposed, but he didn't want to do that. He shrugged and walked to where he had left his horse. He mounted and stared down at her. "All right, Donna. You win. I'll get up a posse and take Dan and his two boys. In the meantime . . . you stay out of sight if they show up. Will you promise to do that?"

She hesitated for a long time. At last she nodded unwillingly.

He turned his horse and rode back the way he had come. He frowned worriedly, hoping what he was doing was right. Donna was in danger. There was little doubt of that.

There was also little doubt that she'd not be much safer in protective custody. The only way she'd really be safe was with all three Radeks lodged in jail. But they'd not be easy to take. They sure as hell weren't going to be easy to take.

Donna watched the sheriff leave with mixed feelings. She was angry, but she was also very much afraid. She knew she was no match for the Radeks. She also knew that she would have no help. Sands had undoubtedly kept going. He was probably out of the country now, perhaps as much as a hundred miles away.

And Varra . . . she was even more afraid of Varra than she was of the Radek clan.

She began to shiver slightly. She raised her head and scanned the valley and the surrounding hills. Suddenly she left the fire and disappeared into the timber on the hillside. She hadn't seen anything. But she had suddenly felt. . . .

What had she felt? It was something she couldn't name, a sense of danger, an uneasy fear.

Silently she climbed the hill, staying on either rock or soft humus until she had gone a quarter mile. Then she stopped, froze, and listened carefully.

She heard voices approaching from across the valley. Cautiously she climbed a pine until she could see across the meadow. She saw Dan Radek and his two sons riding toward the gutted buildings immediately below.

She held her breath, and froze. She saw them pause, saw them quest around briefly for some sign of her.

Then the three went on, and disappeared onto the timbered hillside beyond the fire.

Donna stayed in the tree for a long, long time. Timidly, then, she climbed back to the ground. She made her way cautiously down the hill. Dan and his sons had picked up Varra's trail again, she supposed. And today they'd follow it.

But if they expected Varra to leave the country, they were in for a surprise. They'd have found him as quickly if they'd stayed at home. Varra wanted them even more than they wanted him.

She sat down beside the fire and stared bleakly into it. She thought of Sands, and for an instant her expression softened. Why couldn't it have been different, she wondered. Why couldn't she have met Sands under different circumstances?

Her mouth firmed impatiently. She was mooning like a schoolgirl, she told herself. Sands was gone. She'd never see him again. And even if he hadn't gone, there could be no future with someone like him. He was an escaped convict, a wanted man. Sooner or later someone was going to recognize him. And then he'd be going back—to Yuma—to a sentence longer than it had originally been because of his escape.

She had part of her revenge, she thought. Bert Radek and Jess were dead. Why, then, did she feel no elation, no satisfaction, no joy?

She got up and wandered among the blackened ruins moodily. For the briefest instant she almost wished the Radeks would return, catch her and put an end to it.

She shook her head determinedly. This was no way to feel. She'd charted her course and she'd go through with it to the bitter end.

She returned to the fire, stared at it for several moments, then crossed to the partially erected building and picked up the axe. She began to notch a log, and though the chips did not fly as fast as when Sands had held the axe, she handled it well.

She worked steadily throughout the morning. Sometimes she thought of Sands, of the way he looked, of the steady way his eyes had held hers at times. Sometimes she thought of her father, whom she remembered well or of her mother, whom she remembered not at all.

But however she tried, her thoughts always returned to the present, to the terror that was ahead for her, to the somber guilt she knew was hers.

She asked herself if she would undo the damage she had done, and knew if it was possible, she would. She was sorry she had obtained Varra's release. She was sorry that Bert and Jess Radek were dead.

She kept her rifle close, and at frequent intervals would stop, and listen intently, and study the valley and the hillsides surrounding it.

Noon came, and passed. In mid-afternoon, she heard a noise on the hillside immediately beyond the remains of the house.

She hurried into the partially built cabin, and rested

her rifle on the topmost log. She waited, trembling.

Sands rode out of the timber. He rode straight to her and dismounted wearily.

She said breathlessly, "I thought you'd gone. I thought I'd never see you again."

He grinned. "I told you I'd finish this cabin. Got anything to eat?"

"I'll fix something right away." She hurried to the fire, aware that her face was flushed with pleasure at his return. She busied herself adding wood to the coals, making preparations for a meal.

Sands took the harness off his horse, picketed him, then threw his saddle onto the other one. He asked, "Ever try riding harness for a night and day?"

She turned her head and smiled. For an instant their glances locked.

She said, "Jess Radek was killed last night. He was killed right here."

"Varra's not wasting time."

"Neither are the Radeks. They're trailing him now."

He grinned bleakly at the irony. "They'll trail him straight to their own ranchhouse. Varra wants them as bad as they want him." He tied the horse he had just finished saddling and came to the fire. He sprawled out wearily and watched her, his eyes sober and serious.

At last he asked, "What's going to happen now? It sounds as if things were moving pretty fast."

She nodded. "The sheriff wanted to take me into protective custody."

153

"Why? Because of Varra? I thought he blamed me. . . ."

She said, "Not because of Varra. Because of the Radeks."

"You mean they'd hurt a woman?"

She laughed bitterly. "Do you think a thing like that matters to Dan Radek? I'm a reminder to him—of my mother. I remind him that he lost her to my father. He'd like to see me dead. If Varra hadn't shot Jess when he did last night I'd be dead right now."

Sands stared at her unbelievingly. A spark of anger began to glitter in his eyes. He studied her face, seeing for the first time the bruise Will Purdy had noticed earlier. "Did he do that to you?"

She nodded. Sands didn't speak, but his eyes were smoldering. The fact that they were gave Donna a sudden, warm feeling she had not known for months. He cared, at least, what happened to her.

She smiled as she handed him his plate. Then she got up and walked away from the fire, down to the stream where she stopped. She was a fool. She was behaving like a schoolgirl. She was letting herself fall in love with this man, this killer whom she had bribed out of Yuma Prison. In doing so she was courting disaster and worse heartbreak than she yet had known.

He'd be gone in a day or two. She'd never see him again. He'd probably end up, sooner or later, back in Yuma. Or in some other prison.

She turned her head and looked at him. He was sitting crosslegged on the ground beside the fire, eating ravenously.

And suddenly she didn't care. She knew that, what-ever he had done, he was not like Varra, or like Radek. He would never be like that.

If he would take her when he left, then she would go with him. If he would not, she would wait, and hope that someday he would return. In the meantime, she would do whatever had to be done to make sure he was not hurt, or captured and returned to Yuma to serve out his time.

A certain serenity was apparent in her face as she returned to the fire.

She had set in motion the forces of terror and of death. They were out of her control. But, she discov-ered, she had stopped hating the Radek family.

Her hope for the future extended over a period no longer than the next few days. But she wouldn't waste what time was left. She took his plate and cup and carried them to the stream to wash them. And she felt his eyes upon her all the way.

Chapter Seventeen

Will Purdy did not see the Radeks, nor did they see him. They entered the valley over the timbered ridge lying to the west of it, and he left by the road.

He was not particularly proud of himself, although there was a bit of defiance in him too. He felt as though he was beween two fires, and the feeling angered him.

Donna had started it with her insane thirst for

revenge. She had brought Sands back and the killer with him. He frowned puzzledly.

A killer. You could hire killers for a price. But could you hire men like this one, who struck like a wounded rattler again and again? The man, whoever he was, seemed to have almost a personal stake in what he was doing to the Radek clan.

His frown deepened as he pondered that. Assuming he did have a personal stake, who could he be?

A name came into his thoughts immediately, a name from out of the past. Max Varra. But Varra was in Yuma and no one ever escaped from there.

Or did they? Donna had sold her cattle before she left. She must have had a thousand dollars or more. A thousand dollars would open a lot of doors. Perhaps even the double barred doors inside the grim walls of Yuma Territorial Prison.

He kicked his horse into a trot. There was only one thing he could do now. Get up a posse. Put the remaining three Radeks in jail. And let the killer come to them.

Donna would be safe if he did that. The Radeks would be safer than they now were, trailing a killer who could ambush them at any time. And he'd have a chance at the killer himself.

He kept his horse at a steady trot all the way back to town. He rode down the steady grade to the center of town and dismounted in front of the jail. He stared up the street.

In mid-morning, it was almost deserted. A woman

came out of Delaney's store, carrying a package. A boy with a sling shot was peppering the hotel sign. Two dogs circled each other in the middle of the street, bristling and showing each other their teeth.

Will Purdy tied his horse. He blinked his eyes and thought longingly of the leather-covered couch inside the jail. If he could only sleep, he thought. But he knew there wasn't time.

He walked across the dusty street to the Ace-High saloon. He went inside and crossed to the bar. Ward Bauer brought him a beer and stood looking at him worriedly. "You look like you'd been up all night."

"I have." Purdy sipped the beer. He supposed it would make him sleepy. But maybe it would also take away some of his aching weariness.

He turned his head and looked around the room. Over in the corner, Hughie Sills, the town drunk, was sleeping with his head down on the table. A couple of cowboys were playing two-handed poker for matches at another table. The two glanced up and nodded at him.

The swinging doors opened and John Delaney came in. He crossed to the bar and looked at Bauer. "Gimme a beer, Ward."

He turned his head and stared at the sheriff. "Find out who broke into my store the other night?"

Purdy nodded. "I think it was the same man that killed Bert and Jess Radek, John. I'll know in a day or two."

Delaney sipped his beer. Purdy said, "Can you drop

things long enough to go out with a posse, John?"

"Why, I guess I could. You want me to help catch that killer—the one you think broke into my store?"

Purdy shook his head. "I want to jail the Radek bunch for beating Donna and threatening her. Besides, I figure that with them in jail for bait, the killer will come to me."

There was a moment's silence. Delaney studied the beer sitting on the bar in front of him. At last he said, "I'm pretty busy, Will. I don't think I ought to go."

Fleeting anger touched the sheriff's thoughts. He said, "A minute ago, you thought you could."

"That was when . . ." He stopped, frowning lightly, still staring at his beer. "I'm too busy, Will. Get someone else."

"Scared of the Radeks, John?"

"Aren't you scared, Will? You know Dan Radek and those kids of his as well as I do."

Will Purdy stared at him steadily, his anger smoldering in his eyes. He said, "I'm not asking now, John. I'm telling you. Go get yourself a horse and a sack of grub. Meet me at the jail at noon."

Behind the bar, Ward Bauer stared uneasily from the sheriff to Delaney and back again. Will turned his head. "You too, Ward. Close the saloon and meet me at the jail at noon."

Ward was as silent as Delaney. He stared at the bar in front of him for a long time before he raised his eyes. Then he said, "I saw Dan ride down the street last night with Lew and Frank and with Jess lying face down across his saddle. I saw Dan Radek's face. I don't want to be with the bunch that tries to take Dan and his boys because they aren't going to let anyone take them, Will. Not until they've caught up with the man who shot Bert and Jess."

Purdy said bleakly, softly, "Ward, neither you nor John has got a choice. Either you go with me, or I'll file charges against you for your refusal to go."

Delaney spoke without turning his head. "File 'em, Will. I'd a hell of a lot rather pay a fine for refusing you than I'd face Dan Radek the way he's feeling now. He'll fight you, Will. You'll have to kill him and his two boys before you can bring 'em in."

"Not if I've got a posse. Not if he knows he hasn't got a chance." He said the words but he knew they weren't true even as he uttered them. Dan Radek would fight, no matter what the odds.

Delaney said, "Besides, I think your charge is weak. He might threaten Donna, but he wouldn't hurt her."

Purdy stared at him pityingly. "You know better than that. He was getting ready to kill her when Jess was shot."

"That's still a pretty thin charge to kill a man for. People will say you're setting yourself above the court. The whole country knows Donna blames Dan for old Jake's death. But she's in the wrong, Will. A jury acquitted him."

Will laughed bitterly. "Sure, the jury acquitted Dan

because Dan bribed witnesses. But he did it. You know it and so do I."

"Maybe. But I'm not going to risk my neck butting into Dan Radek's quarrels." Delaney finished his beer and dropped a nickel on the bar. He stepped away, stared at the sheriff for a moment, then turned and went toward the door.

Purdy watched him go, scowling at his back. Behind the bar, Ward Bauer moved away and began to polish glasses, not looking at Will.

The sheriff stared at the two cowboys. He knew they had been listening because neither of the two would look at him. Suddenly the one with the cards slammed them down on the table. The two got up and headed for the door.

Purdy hesitated, on the point of calling out to them. Then, with a little shrug, he let them go. They'd heard him refused by Delaney and Bauer. They knew how helpless he was, and they would refuse him too.

He finished his beer wearily and went outside. He stood in the sun for a moment uncertainly.

People wanted law, he thought sourly, but not if they occasionally had to risk their own hides in support of it. They wanted to pay someone else to take all the risks.

He knew he hadn't a chance of taking the three Radeks by himself. He'd have to wait—either until Varra got them all, or until one of them got Varra instead.

Donna would just have to surrender herself, It was the only way she could be safe.

He stalked angrily back toward the jail. He was aware of the unfairness of the position he was in. In no way had he ever done less than could normally be expected of him. He had brought Dan Radek in and had charged him with the death of Jake Tate. Years before he had arrested Varra on Dan Radek's evidence. He had tried to catch Sands the other day. If he had arrested no one for burning Donna's buildings it was because he had no evidence.

But realizing the unfairness of his position in no way altered it. He still felt responsible for Donna's safety. And she wasn't safe as long as the Radek clan was free.

He stared reluctantly at his horse, tied in front of the jail. He untied the reins and mounted wearily. He was going to have to return to Donna's place. He was going to have to persuade her to leave the country for a while, or bring her in.

He rode out of town, up the uncrowded, dusty street, and he could feel the eyes of the townspeople on his back as he did. He cursed softly, helplessly under his breath.

The ride back up into the high country seemed three times as long as it ever had before. However he tried to stay awake, he could not. He dozed in the saddle, awakening often, but always dozing off again.

It was late afternoon before he reached the place. Donna was still alone, he saw, but he also noted that the walls of the cabin had risen by at least two feet.

Sands had returned, he supposed, and was now hiding up on the timbered hillside, waiting until he had gone. But he didn't care about Sands right now, even though he knew Sands had probably escaped from Yuma at the same time Varra had. There was time for Sands later.

He dismounted, and stared down at Donna's defiant face. "Have the Radeks been back?"

She nodded. "They came just after you left this morning. I went up on the hillside and hid like you told me to. But they were more interested in trailing than in me, because they left right away."

"Did they pick up Varra's trail?"

She nodded, then stopped herself. For an instant her eyes were panicky. Then they blazed at him.

He grinned humorlessly. "I thought that was who it was. How'd you get him out?"

She clamped her lips tightly together and glared at him. He said, "I'm going to give you a choice. You can leave the country, now, and not come back until this is all over. Or you can come into town with me."

"I won't do either one!"

"Oh yes you will." He stared at her implacably. "I can arrest you as an accessory in the murders of Bert and Jess. Or I can arrest you on suspicion of jailbreaking. One way or another I'm going to get you away from here. I can't raise a posse to go after the Radeks and it would be stupid for me to try going after them by myself. So I've got no choice. And I'm not going to have you killed."

She glanced helplessly toward the hillside, as though expecting help. Purdy followed her glance and saw Sands come striding out of the trees. Sands said, "Voices carry well up here. I heard what you said, sheriff."

Sands had a revolver stuffed into his belt. He carried a rifle in his hand.

Purdy studied his face critically. It was a hard face, and competent, but there was neither brutality nor treachery in it. The sheriff asked, "You come out of Yuma with Varra?"

Sands nodded. "But don't get any ideas of sending me back. I'm not going back."

Purdy didn't press the point. He and Sands watched each other warily for several moments. At last Sands said, "If you need some help, sheriff . . . well, I'll help you out for a day or two. I don't like men who beat women very much."

Purdy stared at him. He wanted to refuse because he didn't intend to feel obligated to an escaped criminal. Yet he desperately needed help. Sands was offering him a chance to prevent more killings by throwing the Radeks into jail.

He nodded briefly. "All right." He switched his glance to Donna. "You come along with us. I'll leave you with Mrs. Delaney in town."

Sands walked to where his horse was tied. He mounted, then rode out into the meadow and roped the other one. He led him back and saddled him.

Donna killed the fire. She glanced around at the

temporary camp for a moment, at the partially erected cabin. Then she mounted without a word.

Purdy led out, and Sands followed him. Donna Tate brought up the rear.

The problem was far from solved, Purdy realized. He wanted the Radeks but not yet at the price of deliberately killing them. Taking them without killing might be difficult, if not impossible.

Not that they didn't deserve killing. The list of Dan Radek's crimes was long for a man who still was free. He had hired Varra to kill one of his neighbors ten years before. He had hanged Jake Tate despite the fact that he had been acquitted for it. Purdy suspected that he was guilty of killing a cowboy named Duke Lester a couple of months before, although he hadn't been able to pin it on him. And he had burned Donna's buildings as a spiteful act of anger and revenge.

Knowing these things and proving them were as far apart as night and day. And Delaney had been right. If he killed any of the Radeks he'd be accused of setting himself above the court. But if it came to a choice—of being accused of that, or of being killed—he shook his head angrily. He wasn't going to be a target for the Radeks, no matter what.

Chapter Eighteen

Owen Sands jogged behind the sheriff, down along the edge of the meadow and into the timber at the lower end. He noted the way the sheriff's head sagged forward at intervals, only to jerk erect again. The sheriff was beat, he thought.

He turned his head and looked at Donna. Her face showed weariness. It showed discouragement too. But there was another change, one that was almost indefinable. Her face seemed softer than it ever had before. Her mouth was full and relaxed, no longer compressed by hatred and thirst for revenge.

In one respect, he thought wryly, they were just alike. For a year or more after his conviction, he had wanted vengeance too. Against the family of James Trask, one of whom had deliberately take the gun out of the dead man's hand and let Owen go to Yuma for murdering him.

But time had slaked his thirst for revenge. Now he didn't even want to go back. He never wanted to see the Trask family again. He just wanted to forget.

He smiled reassuringly at Donna and she returned the smile. There was a smudge on her nose, probably from one of the sooty pans. Her hair shone warmly whenever a ray of sun filtered through the timber and touched her head.

He felt a growing need for her, and it showed plainly in his eyes. Her smile faded and color rose into her cheeks. He turned his head and stared at the sheriff's back ahead of him.

A man was as inconsistent as a woman, he thought. A month ago, he had wanted nothing more than to get out of Yuma, to breathe the clean, pure air of freedom, to feel a horse between his knees, to sleep clean beneath the stars. Now he had that freedom and was risking it because of her.

The sun dropped steadily across the western sky. It was setting by the time they reached the forks. Sands called, "Will you try and take them tonight or will you wait for morning?"

The sheriff's head jerked up and turned. His eyes were groggy and glazed. He said harshly, "Tonight. We'll have a better chance in the dark."

Sands nodded. The road dropped steeply away toward town. Light faded from the sky and in the soft gray of dusk, he could see lights dimly begin to sparkle in the town below.

They entered the town and rode down the steep grade toward the center of it. At one of the houses, a tall, two-story gray one, Will Purdy halted his horse. He said, "Go on in, Donna. And do something as a favor to me, will you? Stay in the house and don't let anyone know you're there."

Donna dismounted and Purdy took the reins of her horse from her. She hesitated at the edge of the street, looking up at Sands. Her face was just a blur in the darkness. She said, "Owen. . . ."

He waited, but she did not go on. He said, "Don't

worry. It will come out all right."

"Yes." But there was no conviction in her tone.

He wanted to dismount and take her in his arms. He wanted to reassure her. Instead, he touched the horse's sides with his heels and followed the sheriff down the street.

He turned his head to look back once. He could see her standing there, only a blur in the darkness. But he somehow knew that tears were streaming down her cheeks.

He was a fool, he told himself. He would find women wherever he went. Why should he risk so much for her?

And why should he help this local sheriff take the Radeks? Why, when he could be miles away by morning, and safe, if he started now?

Purdy lived by rules. When this was over, Purdy would send him back. To Yuma. To execution, perhaps, for the killing of the guard.

He stared at Purdy's back almost angrily. He thought, "Guess again, sheriff. If you want to send me back you're going to have to put up a fight."

They stopped in town long enough to eat in the hotel dining-room. Sands could not help noticing the way people looked at Purdy. With a mixture of pity and disapproval. He said, "You don't seem too popular."

The sheriff grunted, "No lawman is when things get tough. They know I've got my tail in a crack. But they're blaming me because I've let two men be murdered in the past two days."

"They won't help you though. Is that it?"

"Not to take the Radeks."

"Why don't you go after Varra then?"

"Because it's a wild goose chase. Because he ain't running away. All he'll do is draw me away from town. Then he'll double back and kill himself another one."

"And you figure if you can get the Radeks in jail, Varra will come to you?"

The sheriff nodded.

They finished eating and got up. They went outside, rode to the stable where they changed horses and dropped off Donna's horse, then rode out of town again, heading west.

Both men were utterly silent all the way to the Radek place. Only when they brought its lights into sight did the sheriff say, "I wish I wasn't so goddam tired. I can't even seem to think."

"Have you a plan for doing this? It's not going to be easy."

The sheriff didn't reply. He swung from his horse and said, "We'd better go from here on foot."

Sands dismounted. Darkness favored them, he realized, but darkness wasn't going to be enough.

He followed the sheriff afoot toward the house, scowling to himself in the darkness. This was like taking a wounded panther with your bare hands, he thought. The three Radeks were as edgy as any wounded animal. They would shoot at the slightest noise. . . .

Furthermore, they thought he was the one who had killed Bert and Jess. They didn't even know about Varra yet.

Wryly he wondered how he could have been stupid enough to get himself into this. Then he remembered the bruise on Donna's face, and felt his anger stir. Yet even with anger stirring him, he could still wonder at himself for stepping into a situation as hopeless as this one was.

A hundred yards from the house, he caught the sheriff's sleeve. He whispered urgently, "What the hell are you going to do? You can't just walk up there and order them to surrender themselves."

Purdy's voice was cold. "That's exactly what I'm going to do."

"Don't be a fool! They'll cut you down before they even know who you are!"

"Maybe." The sheriff stood frozen, neither yielding nor resisting until Sands released his sleeve. Then he stalked silently, stiffly toward the house.

Sands let him go—until his shape faded into the darkness—until the soft, sibilant sounds of the sheriff's careful steps faded from his ears. Then he stooped and removed his boots. The sheriff was a fool, but that didn't mean both of them had to be.

Carrying his boots, angling left to avoid the sheriff ahead of him, Sands ran. He had the rifle in his hands and as he ran, he quietly jacked a cartridge into the chamber. He came up at the rear of the house, moving more carefully so that he wouldn't blunder into anything that might make a noise.

The sheriff would be calling out any minute now. He felt a touch of panic at the thought of the sheriff doing so before he was ready. . . .

He circled the house as carefully as he could. Blinds were drawn over all the windows, perhaps to keep anyone from shooting through them.

He reached the front wall of the house. No one had challenged him yet, which probably meant that all three of the Radeks were inside. And if they were— then it was not as hopeless as it had seemed. Before they could shoot the sheriff, they had to come outside. Or darken the house. Either way, both he and the sheriff would have a few seconds to prepare. . . .

The sheriff's roaring voice made him start violently in spite of himself. The voice bawled, "Dan! Dan Radek! It's Will Purdy! You and your boys come out—without your guns!"

Inside the house, a lamp went out. A second lamp also went out, plunging the place into total darkness. Sands bawled, "Sheriff! Drop!"

He heard a scuffle of movement in the yard, the tinkle of window glass. Almost instantly after that, three guns laid a withering fire across the yard.

Sands held his breath. If the sheriff was killed in that first savage burst of fire . . .

The firing stopped, as suddenly as it had begun. Sands heard the sheriff scrambling along the ground. Purdy reached the corner of the house and stood up, breathing hard. He panted, "Christ! That was a close one!"

With their guns reloaded, the Radeks opened up again. When this volley stopped, the sheriff yelled, "Give up, Dan. Sands ain't the killer. It's Varra! Donna Tate bribed Varra out of Yuma!"

This brought a dead silence from the house. Purdy whispered, "I didn't think they'd cut loose on me like that. I told them who I was."

Sands sat down and put on his boots. He got up again, thinking that this was a Mexican stand-off if he'd ever seen one. Either the Radeks were going to have to come out or he and the sheriff would have to go in.

One thing was sure. Neither he nor the sheriff was going to go inside because that would be committing suicide.

Purdy's breathing had quieted now. He whispered, "I guess that was a damn fool stunt. I knew the Radeks were mean, but I didn't think they'd be ornery enough to shoot me down."

"What are you going to do now?"

"Damned if I know."

Sands whispered, "They've either got to come out or wait for daylight, and I doubt if they've got the patience to wait. Why don't I circle the house? I'll come up on the far side of the door and you come up on this side. When they do come out. . . ." He left the sentence unfinished.

Purdy said, "All right." Weariness was very apparent in his voice. The man was so damned worn out he wasn't even thinking straight, Sands thought.

He faded back into the darkness, calling himself a fool because he didn't get out of here now, while he could. He circled the house.

Stationing themselves on either side of the door was about all they could do, but it certainly didn't assure them of success. One or more of the Radeks could come through a window. If two of them did that—if a third lighted a lamp inside the house and then threw open the door. . . .

He shrugged fatalistically, knowing he could not anticipate everything the Radeks might decide to do. He stooped low each time he passed a window and at last reached the front corner of the house. Perhaps he'd hear them if they did try to come out a window. Provided there was no other noise at the time they did.

He could see the sheriff's dim form on the other side of the door, hugging the wall at his back. The two stood there silently for what seemed an interminable time.

In the utter silence, even his own breathing seemed deafening to Sands. And then, suddenly, he heard movement at his side of the house.

Immediately following that slight sound, he heard Dan Radek's roar, "Now, Frank! Now!"

He whirled toward the corner of the house, his rifle cocked. Light flickered inside the house, immediately streaming through a window half a dozen feet from him. He heard a hand fumbling at the door. . . .

He plunged, running, toward the corner of the

house. The door flung open behind him, throwing a square of light onto the soapsuds-whitened ground in front of it.

He struck a body as he reached the corner of the house. The impact was almost stunning in its force and both he and the man he'd collided with sprawled on the ground beyond. A shot racketed almost in his ear and he felt the heat of the powder blast on his cheek.

He couldn't tell which of the Radeks he'd struck. But he knew the man was powerful. He grappled savagely, trying to hold onto his rifle with one hand.

A revolver clipped him on the cheekbone, bringing a sudden rush of blood. He heard another shot, but this one seemed to come from far away.

He released the rifle and groped for his antagonist's throat. He felt it, thick and hairy beneath his hands.

The gun blasted again, and this bullet seared along his ribs. The next would kill him, he thought, if he didn't get hold of that gun. . . .

He released the throat and groped for the gun. He wished there was more light. They had rolled behind the corner of the house and were in total darkness now.

He got one hand on the gun. It fired, and the hammer came down on the skin between his thumb and forefinger.

It hurt like hell. And it made his anger towering. He wrenched the gun away, still hanging from his bleeding hand, and brought it savagely around. He felt it strike something solid.

The man relaxed suddenly. Sands tore himself free and scrambled to his feet. The gun hung from his bleeding hand like a rattlesnake with its fangs in him. With the other hand, he thumbed the hammer back, releasing it.

Dan Radek, his head bleeding, was scrambling toward him, rising as he did. Sands kicked out at him.

His booted foot struck Dan in the face but it only slowed him momentarily. Sands brought the gun down savagely.

It made a dull, sodden sound as it struck Dan's skull. The man collapsed on his face in the dust.

Still holding the gun, Sands whirled. Purdy was struggling with Frank at the far corner of the house. As Sands watched, Frank flung the sheriff away and raised his gun.

Sands fired unthinkingly. The bullet caught Frank in the shoulder and whirled him bodily around. His gun fell from his nerveless fingers to the ground.

The sheriff got stiffly to his feet. His face was covered with blood and dust. He spat blood at the ground.

Sands stepped toward him. As he reached the door, he turned his head. Lew Radek was lying just inside the door on his back. His eyes were open, staring. . . . There was a neat, bluish hole exactly in the center of his forehead.

Sands suddenly remembered the single shot that had seemed to come from far away. Varra had struck again. And now only Dan and Frank were left.

Chapter Nineteen

Out in the darkness Varra's rifle spat wickedly again. The bullet struck the log wall behind Frank, tearing loose a shower of splinters before it ricocheted away, whining, into the night.

Frank, his face contorted with pain, yelled, "It's Varra! For God's sake, don't let him get me too!"

The sheriff started to speak but Sands caught his sleeve. He looked at Frank callously. "Why not? After what you and your old man have done. . . ."

"I never touched Donna! It was pa!"

"What about her father? Was that pa too?"

Frank was sweating heavily. His face had a grayish color to it. He looked down with horror at the blood running off his finger tips. He said, "For the love of God. . . ."

The sheriff said "Sands . . . we. . . !"

Sands' voice was like the sibilant swish of an arrow in flight. "Shut up! Wait!" He stared implacably at Frank. "What about her father, Frank? If I was you, I'd open up. Varra's probably taking another bead on you right now."

Frank's head swiveled frantically and he stared out into the darkness. He shouted, "All right! We helped him do that—all of us. He said Jake had killed Lee. . . ."

Sands leaped for the door. He struck the lamp with a sweeping arm and it crashed against the wall, smashing, going out. He went back outside again.

The sheriff was helping Frank toward the door. Sands went to where Dan Radek lay. He stooped and got him beneath the armpits. He dragged him into the house, straightened and closed the door.

It was pitch black now. He couldn't see anything. He said, "You can quit worrying about what happened here tonight, sheriff. You heard what Frank just said. You can bring 'em to trial again."

"Huh uh. They can't be tried for the same crime twice." The sheriff was going from one window to the next, lowering the blinds. When he had finished, he struck a match.

Sands found the lamp and the sheriff lighted it. He heard a sodden crash and swung his head. Frank had collapsed and was lying on the floor.

Sands crossed to him. He could see no rise and fall in Frank's chest. Kneeling, he picked up the man's wrist. After a moment, he turned his head. "He's dead."

"Then all we got is Dan. And if we don't get him to town before it gets light, Varra will kill him too."

There was shock in the sheriff's face as he glanced at Owen Sands. He said, "Frank would have killed me if you hadn't shot when you did."

Sands didn't reply. He crossed to a small table beside the stove and picked up a bucket half filled with water. He took a drink out of the bucket, then dumped the rest into Dan Radek's face. Dan choked, gasped a couple of times, then opened his eyes and sat up.

He stared numbly at his two dead sons. He stared at Sands with hatred so vitriolic that his glance seemed to strike almost like a blow.

Purdy said, "Get up, Dan. We're going back to town."

"What about them? You got to bury 'em."

"Later. If we don't get you to town before daylight, Varra's going to kill you too."

Dan began to curse. Sands went to him and cuffed him on the mouth. "Shut up. Your son talked before he died. He admitted hanging Jake Tate."

"You're a liar! He wouldn't. . . ."

Purdy said, "Maybe not, but he did."

"You can't try me twice. No matter what he said."

Purdy said wearily, "No. We can't try you twice. But don't push me, Dan. Or I'll just let Varra have you." He rummaged around the kitchen until he found a length of light rope. While Sands held a gun on Dan, he tied the man's hands behind him.

Sands blew out the lamp. He opened the door and stepped outside. He crossed at a run to the barn, gun in hand, and went inside. He saddled a horse for Dan and led him back to the house.

He boosted Dan to the saddle. The sheriff took the reins of Dan's horse and led out at a fast trot toward town. Sands brought up the rear.

Now that it was over, he realized how close it had been. If, instead of colliding with Dan at the corner of the house, he had plunged past it an instant before Dan reached it. . . . The end would have been very different. Dan would have killed him and caught the sheriff from the rear.

Alternately trotting their horses and loping, they reached the edge of town as dawn began to gray the sky. They went directly to the jail, dismounted and went inside without lighting a lamp. Purdy took Dan back to a cell and locked him in.

Returning, he looked at Sands. His eyes were heavy, his face slack with weariness. "Now I've got to try and get Varra."

"Wait for him here, sheriff. He'll come. Dan's the one he wanted most."

"I'd like to believe that. I could sure use a little sleep."

"He'll come, sheriff. I traveled all the way from Yuma with him and I know."

"I. . . . You reckon you could stay awake for a little while? If I don't get some sleep. . . ."

"Go ahead, sheriff. I'll stay awake."

Purdy nodded. He looked half asleep already. He said, "I'll get someone to go out there after Frank and Lew." He crossed to the door and went outside.

He was gone about fifteen minutes. When he returned, he went immediately to the leather-covered couch and flopped down on it. He was almost instantly asleep.

Sands got up and paced restlessly back and forth. He was tired himself, but he knew he wouldn't sleep even if he tried. He thought of Donna and hoped she'd had sense enough to stay where the sheriff had left her—at Delaney's house.

Her revenge was now almost complete, he thought. All of Dan's sons were dead. Only Dan remained and as long as Varra remained free, even Dan's hope of life was slim.

He went into the cellblock and stared at the window of Dan's cell. It was small and barred heavily. It was also higher than a man's head. In order to get at Dan, Varra would have to stand on something outside of it.

He returned to the office, ignoring Dan's murderous stare. He went outside and around to the side of the building where Dan's cell was. There was nothing here Varra could stand on.

He went back inside and closed the door. Varra would have no way of knowing which cell Dan was in. It followed, therefore, that when Varra came after Dan he'd come in the front door.

He put a chair against the wall, sat in it and tilted it back. He stared directly at the door. Purdy began to snore heavily.

The hours dragged past. Occasionally, Sands rolled a cigarette and smoked it, tossing it at the brass spittoon when it was finished.

The sheriff awakened about four in the afternoon. He sat up, rubbing his eyes and his heavily whiskered face. His eyes were blurred with his sudden awakening.

Sands grinned at him. "Feel better now?"

Purdy got up and walked to the front window. He stared into the street. He grunted, "Too soon to tell. Anything happen?"

"Not a thing. Want something to eat?"

Yawning, the sheriff turned. "Yeah. Why don't you go down to the hotel and tell 'em to send over three trays."

"Think you can stay awake while I'm gone?"

"I'll try." Purdy grinned.

Sands crossed to the door and went outside. The sky was clouded over and the air had a still, hot feeling to it. He glanced at the piled up clouds over the mountains south of town. It was going to rain up there tonight, he thought. It was really going to rain.

He went along the street to the hotel. He went through the lobby and dining-room to the kitchen. The cook glanced at him questioningly and Sands said, "The sheriff wants you to send three trays over to the jail."

The man nodded. Sands returned to the street.

Something was different down there in front of the jail. He frowned, for an instant unable to place exactly what it was. Then, suddenly, he knew. Four horses were tied to the rail in front of the jail instead of three.

He began to run. He had taken no more than half a dozen steps when he heard the shot.

He yanked his gun from its holster and thumbed the hammer back. Varra must have been watching the jail all day. And the minute Sands had left. . . .

The door of the jail slammed open and Varra came running out. He glanced down the street, then up. He saw Sands and raised his rifle . . .

180

Sands dived for a doorway. He ducked into it as the rifle slug struck the wall, tearing a gouge in it, throwing up a shower of splinters.

Sands cursed softly beneath his breath. He stuck his head out, yanked it back as another of Varra's bullets smashed the glass beside his head.

The distance was too far for his revolver, he realized. Even if he exposed himself to Varra's rifle fire, he probably couldn't hit the man.

He poked his head out again. Varra was mounting. Sands stepped out and took a deliberate bead on Varra's horse. He fired.

The horse went down. Varra jumped clear, then knelt and aimed carefully. Sands ducked back.

When he dared poke his head out again, he saw that Varra had another horse, the one Sands had saddled for Dan early this morning. He was already heading downstreet toward the edge of town.

Varra was spurring recklessly. The street was deserted. Everyone who had been on it had ducked to safety at the first sound of gunfire. Sands ran toward the jail.

He burst inside. The sheriff lay across the couch, a bleeding bruise on the side of his head. Sands ran across the office and into the cellblock at the rear.

Dan Radek lay spread out on the floor. There was a hole between his eyes. It was over then. The last of the Radeks was dead.

He returned to the office. The sheriff's eyes were open and he was trying to sit up. Sands helped him.

It took several moments for remembrance of what had happened to come to the sheriff's eyes. Then he asked, "Dan?"

"He's dead."

The sheriff stared at the floor between his feet. He said heavily, "I dozed off. I came awake just as Varra swung his gun."

He got up and started for the cellblock. He staggered and would have fallen except that Sands caught and steadied him.

Purdy went into the cellblock and stared at Dan's body with glazed eyes. Sands said softly, "Varra will be a hundred miles from here by morning. If we're going to get him, we've got to start right now."

"We?"

Sands said, "It'll take you at least an hour to get a posse up. That hour will kill any chance you've got of catching him."

"All right. Go down to the stable and get two fresh horses."

Sands headed for the door. He ran down the street toward the livery barn, leading the two horses he and the sheriff had ridden last night.

He was a fool, he thought. What he ought to do was get one horse for himself and ride out of town tonight. The sheriff would be too busy for a day or two pursuing Varra to worry about catching him. By the time Purdy caught Varra, or gave up, he could be two hundred miles away, and safe.

He went into the stable. The same man he'd sold the

packhorse to a couple of days before was there. Sands said, "The sheriff wants a couple of horses. Hurry up."

The man looked at him intently, then hurried toward the corral in the rear. Sands unsaddled the two horses he had been leading and took their bridles off. He waited impatiently.

He seemed to have made his choice, he thought, and it probably was wrong. Yet he discovered he had no regrets. In a sense, the fact that Varra was free was a burden on his conscience as much as it was one on Donna Tate's. If he wasn't caught, Varra would kill again and again. The man was like a mad dog, loose.

The stableman hurried to him, leading two horses. Sands saddled one while the stableman saddled the other. When they had finished, he mounted one and, leading the other, rode up the street to the jail.

Purdy was waiting for him, looking sick but steady enough. He mounted.

Sands led out of town in the direction Varra had gone.

He picked up the trail easily where it left the road, followed it as it turned, circled the town and headed south. He turned his head and stared at Purdy, concern showing suddenly in his eyes. "He's heading for Donna's place."

"It doesn't matter. She's at Delaney's."

"You sure of that?"

"I can make sure. You stay with the trail and I'll meet you on the other side of town." Purdy whirled his horse and sank his spurs. He pounded back toward town.

Sands kicked his horse's sides, urging him to a lope. There was a worried frown on his face.

Varra never forgot anything. He had wanted Donna all the way from Yuma. Now, with his revenge complete, he was going after her.

Chapter Twenty

Varra's trail made a wide circle of the town. Then it led straight up the steep ridge until it reached the first switchback. Thereafter it followed the road.

Sands paused briefly where the trail entered the road. Varra had been spurring his horse mercilessly. The tracks were deeply indented, and in places showed where the horse had scrambled frantically.

He stared impatiently back at the town. He saw the sheriff's horse coming up the street above Delaney's tall gray house.

The sheriff's uplifted face looked white in the distance. Behind Sands there was a low rumble of thunder, a rumble that rolled ponderously across the darkening sky.

Sands guessed it was about four-thirty. In two and a half hours it would be dark. In less time than that rain might obscure Varra's trail. The sheriff pounded up the road. Sands knew what he was going to say even before he said it. "She's gone. Mrs. Delaney said she went back home."

Sands cursed softly under his breath. Why in the hell hadn't she stayed where she was supposed to stay? If she had, she'd be safe right now. As it was. . . .

He waited a full minute for the sheriff's horse to catch its breath. Then he went on, his face set angrily. Yet there was more than anger in his eyes. There was fear. He knew what Varra would do to Donna when he found her at the burned-out ranch.

Mercilessly he drummed his heels against his horse's sides and whipped the animal's rump with the ends of the reins, wishing he had some spurs.

Behind him, the sheriff rode silently, his face worried.

The clouds were almost black. They drove swiftly along on a rising wind, sometimes no higher than the mountain tops. A drop of stinging rain struck Owen Sands in the face.

He forced the horse to lope and kept him loping all the way to the fork in the road. Here he halted unwillingly.

The horse stood, head down, sides heaving. Sands stared at the sheriff's face. He said, "He'll. . . . I had to fight him all the way up here from Yuma to keep him away from her. He's been in prison ten years and he hasn't had a woman in all that time."

Purdy's face was grim, filled with sympathy and with deep concern. He said reassuringly, "We'll get there in time. He can't be more than ten or fifteen minutes ahead of us."

"That's long enough to. . . ."

"Take it easy, Sands."

"Yeah." The word was bitter, filled with helpless rage.

"It won't help to kill your horse."

"I know that. That's why I stopped." He looked down at his horse, wanting to force him to go on, knowing he'd make it faster in the long run if he gave the horse a couple more minutes to rest.

"Sands."

"What?"

"Colorado's a state now. They'll have to extradite you. If I was to ask the Governor to refuse. . . ." He looked at Sands almost defensively. "Well hell, you didn't have to help me take the Radeks. You could have been long gone if you'd wanted to."

Sands didn't look at him. He was afraid to believe. . . .

"Would you stay here if you had a job? I've been thinking I ought to have a deputy—someone younger than me."

Sands met his glance suddenly. "You're damned right I'd stay."

"All right. Let's go get Varra then."

Sands started his horse up the road again. He drummed on the animal's sweating sides.

The ride to Donna's place had never seemed so long before. The sky grew ever darker as they rode. The clouds now obscured the mountain tops. Gray, ragged wisps of cloud whirled along the mountain sides, sometimes reaching all the way to the canyon floor. It began to rain, slowly at first, in stinging, tiny drops.

But as it continued, the rain grew heavier, the drops larger, until the land ahead was blotted out by drifting, swirling pillars of it.

Owen's horse lost his footing on the slick road, righted himself, then slid again with all four legs stiffly braced. Sands cursed angrily beneath his breath. He pulled the horse off the road, onto the grass at the side of it. He did not slow down.

They reached the lower end of the meadow in which Donna's gutted buildings lay. Sands' horse was running hard. The sheriff was no more than a hundred and fifty feet behind, but was out of sight in the whipping rain.

Already Sands was soaked to the skin. Water ran in a steady stream off the brim of his hat in front and blew back into his streaming face. His hands felt numb from cold.

He strained his eyes, trying to see through the curtain of driving rain. The burnt buildings appeared ahead of him almost before he realized it.

His glance took in Varra's horse, standing ground-tied beside the partially erected cabin. His eyes saw the deeply indented tracks leading to where the heaving horse now stood. His mind knew a sudden surge of relief. Varra must have arrived just now. He must have arrived since the rain began. He could not have been here more than a few minutes at most.

He roared, "Donna!" and flung himself, running, from his horse. He lost his footing as he struck the muddy ground and went down in a heap.

The rifle roared from the partially built cabin. The bullet buzzed over Owen's head and struck his horse, immediately behind. The animal grunted heavily, then began to buck. He bucked down toward the stream, but he never got that far. He collapsed to the ground and lay kicking helplessly.

The rifle roared again. This bullet showered Owen with mud. He heard Donna scream. He was rolling, scrambling, trying to avoid the next bullet when it came.

The sheriff thundered up behind him. He did not check his horse but ran him almost to the cabin wall before he left the saddle in a leap that sent him sliding, crashing against the bottom log.

Varra's head and shoulders came up over the wall as he tried to bring his rifle to bear on the sheriff. Sands clawed to his feet.

His hands were covered with mud, and slick. His gun which had been in his hand was probably jammed with mud, he thought, and would blow up if he fired it.

Varra, hanging over the top of the log wall, brought the muzzle of his rifle down. Sands, scrambling toward him, held his breath. Then Varra seemed to lose his balance. He began to slide back and the rifle muzzle raised.

The gun discharged, but the bullet slammed into the ground a dozen feet beyond the place the sheriff lay.

Sands plunged through the door opening, into the small enclosure he had built. Donna had both arms locked around Varra's legs below the knee. It was her weight that had pulled him back, that had saved the sheriff's life.

Varra struck the ground, furiously swinging the rifle barrel at Donna's head. It grazed her head and swung, bearing now directly on Sands. Flame shot from its muzzle.

Sands felt a blow like the kick of a horse on his shoulder. He felt himself flung helplessly back, through the doorway to sprawl on the muddy ground outside. He caught a glimpse of the sheriff, rounding the corner at a run.

Varra plunged out of the doorway at the same instant, collided violently with the sheriff and went on, to lose his footing and fall, face downward, in the mud.

Sands clawed toward him, feeling dizziness and weakness mounting in his head. He reached Varra and swung his muddy, fisted revolver in a savage arc.

Varra's elbow struck him in the mouth and rolled him aside. But the man was groggy from the blow. His eyes seemed partly glazed.

Purdy roared, "Get away from him! Get away!"

Sands rolled away. The sheriff's rifle roared.

The bullet drove Varra, who had partially raised himself, backward to sprawl to the ground a second time. The sheriff ran toward Sands, yelling. "You hit? How bad?"

Sands got to his hands and knees, the revolver still in his hand. He straightened on his knees, shaking his head to clear it so that everything would stop whirling around. He saw Varra stir, saw him raise himself and bring the rifle to bear on the sheriff's back.

He raised the revolver and fired unthinkingly.

The bullet struck Varra squarely in the chest. For an instant his eyes were unbelieving, as though that small chunk of lead had shattered his belief in his own indestructibility. Then he fell back, his eyes empty, and rolled for a few feet, limply, before he came to rest. There was no longer any movement in his chest.

Sands let the sheriff help him to his feet. He was covered with mud. He could feel the warmth of blood running down his left arm, and, glancing aside at the wound, saw that his shoulder was red with it.

Donna reached him then. Supporting him on opposite sides, she and the sheriff got him inside the doubtful shelter of the four log walls. They eased him to the ground on the side most protected from the wind and rain.

Donna was weeping uncontrollably. Purdy said, "I'll find some dry wood if I can."

He disappeared immediately. Sands heard him crashing through the underbrush on the hillside immediately above.

He looked at Donna's streaming face. Tears were mingling with rain and mud on her cheeks. Her eyes were enormous, staring at him fearfully.

He grinned weakly. "I can move it, so I guess it's not the bone. I'll be all right. And I'll be staying here.

Purdy says he can persuade the Governor not to extradite me. He's even offered me a job."

Carefully she laid her face against his chest. Slowly her sobs quieted.

Sands looked down at her. He raised his right hand and touched her hair.

Yuma Territorial Prison suddenly seemed a thousand miles away. The reality was here, in this place, with this small, determined girl. She raised her head suddenly and smiled. And it was like the sun coming out from behind the clouds.

There was no longer any need for words. Both of them knew that this was the end of hatred and vengeance and despair. But it was a beginning too. Most of all, it was a new beginning for both of them.

Center Point Publishing
600 Brooks Road ● PO Box 1
Thorndike ME 04986-0001 USA

(207) 568-3717

US & Canada:
1 800 929-9108
www.centerpointlargeprint.com